VIRTUAL CRIME.
REAL PUNISHMENT.
TOM CLANCY'S NET FORCE®

*Don't miss any of these exciting adventures
starring the teens of Net Force . . .*

VIRTUAL VANDALS

The Net Force Explorers go head-to-head with a group of teenage pranksters on-line—and find out firsthand that virtual bullets can kill you!

THE DEADLIEST GAME

The virtual Dominion of Sarxos is the most popular wargame on the Net. But someone is taking the game too seriously . . .

ONE IS THE LONELIEST NUMBER

The Net Force Explorers have exiled Roddy—who sabotaged one program too many. But Roddy's created a new "playroom" to blow them away . . .

THE ULTIMATE ESCAPE

Net Force Explorer pilot Julio Cortez and his family are being held hostage. And if the proper authorities refuse to help, it'll be Net Force Explorers to the rescue!

THE GREAT RACE

A virtual space race against teams from other countries will be a blast for the Net Force Explorers. But someone will go to any extreme to sabotage the race—even murder . . .

END GAME

An exclusive resort is suffering Net thefts, and Net Force Explorer Megan O'Malley is ready to take the thief down. But the criminal has a plan to put her out of commission—*permanently* . . .

(continued . . .)

CYBERSPY

A "wearable computer" permits a mysterious hacker access to a person's most private thoughts. It's up to Net Force Explorer David Gray to convince his friends of the danger—before secrets are revealed to unknown spies . . .

SHADOW OF HONOR

Was Net Force Explorer Andy Moore's deceased father a South African war hero or the perpetrator of a massacre? Andy's search for the truth puts every one of his fellow students at risk . . .

PRIVATE LIVES

The Net Force Explorers must delve into the secrets of their commander's life—to prove him innocent of murder . . .

SAFE HOUSE

To save a prominent scientist and his son, the Net Force Explorers embark on a terrifying virtual hunt for their enemies—before it's too late . . .

GAMEPREY

A gamer's convention turns deadly when virtual reality monsters escape their confines—and start tracking down the Net Force Explorers!

DUEL IDENTITY

A member of a fencing group lures the Net Force Explorers to his historical simulation site—where his dream of ruling a virtual nation is about to come true, but only at the cost of their lives . . .

DEATHWORLD

When suicides are blamed on a punk/rock/morbo website, Net Force Explorer Charlie Davis goes onto the site undercover—and unaware of its real danger . . .

HIGH WIRE

The only ring Net Force Explorer Andy Moore finds in a virtual circus is a black market ring—in high-tech weapons software and hardware . . .

COLD CASE

Playing detective in a mystery simulation, Net Force Explorer Matt Hunter becomes the target of a flesh-and-blood killer . . .

RUNAWAYS

Tracking down a runaway friend, Net Force Explorer Megan O'Malley discovers that the web is just as fraught with danger as the streets . . .

CLOAK AND DAGGER

A game of hide-and-seek on the web pits the Net Force Explorers against the CIA . . .

TOM CLANCY'S
NET FORCE®

DEATH MATCH

CREATED BY

Tom Clancy and **Steve Pieczenik**

Written by

Diane Duane

BERKLEY JAM BOOKS, NEW YORK

TOM CLANCY'S NET FORCE: DEATH MATCH

A Berkley Jam Book / published by arrangement with
Netco Partners

PRINTING HISTORY
Berkley Jam edition / July 2003

ISBN: 0-425-18448-X

BERKLEY JAM BOOKS®
Berkley Jam Books are published by The Berkley Publishing Group,
a division of Penguin Group (USA) Inc.,
375 Hudson Street, New York, New York 10014.
BERKLEY JAM and its logo
are trademarks belonging to Penguin Group (USA) Inc.

PRINTED IN THE UNITED STATES OF AMERICA

10 9 8 7 6 5 4 3 2 1

Acknowledgments

We would like to acknowledge the assistance of Martin H. Greenberg, Larry Segriff, Denise Little, John Helfers, Brittiany Koren, Lowell Bowen, Esq., Robert Youdelman, Esq., Danielle Forte, Esq., Dianne Jude and Tom Colgan, our editor. But most important, it is for you, our readers, to determine how successful our collective endeavor has been.

—TOM CLANCY AND STEVE PIECZENIK

1

The score was tied all around, it was four minutes until the end of the third half, and Catie Murray was sitting literally on the edge of her seat, her fists clenched, staring into the gamesphere. All around her, arranged in concentric, nested spheres, hanging in what seemed like floodlit darkness, were the virtual "seemings" of about fifty thousand other people. Most of them were yelling with excitement, though some of them were silent and rigid with tension, and to Catie's amazement, one of these silent ones, sitting next to her, was her brother, Hal, whom she had last noticed being silent sometime in 2009, just before he started learning to talk.

The sphere was transparent, and of full tournament size—ninety meters in diameter. Away down at what was presently the red goal "end," seventeen people were gathered, floating just outside of the safe zone, jostling one another gently as they jockeyed for the best positions or tried to steal a little impetus from one another. They wore shorts and socks and T-shirt "tunics" in their team colors. One group of six wore a truly astonishing lime green with a blue horizontal stripe, another group white with a red chevron, a third group yellow with a pair of black circles emblazoned on each shirt, front and back, like eyes.

Five of the team wearing yellow were currently floating in front of the red "end" zone, marked out in the space by a red hexagonal gridwork of holographic lines, as the other goals were by hexes of green and yellow, at 180 degree angles to this one. The sixth player in yellow was hanging in midair not too far from the wall of the transparent sphere, holding a fluorescent orange ball, slightly smaller than a soccer ball, in both hands. As Catie watched, he let go of it. It hung in the air in front of him, wobbling only slightly. There was a sudden slight burst of pushing and shoving from the players not dressed in yellow as they boosted themselves off one another and toward the man in the end zone—

In a flash the man bent himself almost double, it seemed to Catie, planted his feet against the wall, and hit the ball with his head. Despite the best efforts of all the players of the other teams, it somehow managed to squirt straight through them, though their arms and legs flailed out in an attempt to stop it. There was a roar of satisfaction from parts of the crowd, and much waving of yellow objects, some of them resembling giant inflatable bananas. Still using the impetus from his push, the player who had made the throwback went after it as his teammates also used the curve of the nearby walls to launch themselves in various directions, but not, Catie noticed, at the ball. The other teams were left to chase that for the moment—

"Where are they going?" she whispered. Her brother didn't say a word. Catie glanced at him, but got no response. He was sitting there tensely crouched over with his arms folded, all his attention fixed on a spot around ninety degrees around the sphere from where the team captain had taken the ball out for the throwback. In the center of the sphere, players from all three teams were now tangled up in what to Catie looked like a rugby "scrum"—a shapeless-seeming mess of people trying with all their might either to get at the ball, or to keep others away from it while passing it to another friendly team member. For a moment it was lost among them, invisible in the huddle of bodies and tangle of legs, as people strove for purchase in the near-zero gravity, trying to exploit what acceleration they had leftover from the energy of their last push against the wall, trying to exploit the others' energy for their own uses.

Suddenly the ball emerged, flying out of the tangle at about a thirty-degree angle to Catie's left. A couple of the players in blue freed themselves from the tangle and launched themselves after it, pushing off with their feet against the huddle of other players who were all jammed together in the middle of things. The whole tangle of men and women wavered a little backward in equal-and-opposite reaction as the first two players pushed off. Then the tangle broke up and went after them, players tightening themselves down into "cannonball" configuration to increase their spin, or to improve the results of a push against some other player. One of the players in blue, a big redheaded, long-legged, slender guy, snagged the ball in the bend of his knee, pulled his arms close to his body like a skater, and spun on his longitudinal axis—then, a second later, used the force of his spin to fling the ball away from him, straight at one of his teammates. This one batted it with the flats of both hands down out of the air and kneed it to a third. The third one boosted himself off one of the players in red and white, sending the other one spinning, and hit the ball with his chest, aiming at one of the other two goal hexes, the one glowing yellow almost directly across the sphere from him—

Except it suddenly wasn't the goal anymore. It went dark, and 180 degrees around the sphere from it, and about forty-five degrees up, a different hex was now glowing gold. The other goals had both changed position as well.

Another mad scramble for position began, players "swimming" or cannonballing themselves through the space to get at the walls, where there would be purchase for a good hard push, or contenting themselves with a less vigorous push off other players. Here and there several players gathered together and braced to give a single teammate more mass to push against. The ball was in free fall, no one in possession for the moment, but that was about to change, for the players in yellow had so coordinated their launches that four of them were now converging on the ball from different directions. Other players in green or white were arrowing at them from the walls, folded up with arms wrapped around knees, determined to hit them and throw them off course. One got hit and caromed off toward the wall, but as he went he managed to snag the White-team player who had hit him, adding to his mass temporarily and so slowing the speed at which he was being knocked out of play. For a moment Catie watched with some amusement as the two of them struggled for the best position in which to use the other's vector. Her attention was caught by one of the other Yellow team people, whose T-shirt read 14, as she arched her body so that a White-team forward, aiming for her, missed her by inches. Then 14 Yellow tightened down into cannonball configuration herself, first giving the forward a shove with her feet in passing that simply aided her again in the direction she had originally been going. The white forward flung arms and legs out, spreadeagling, trying to lose some speed, but the move was too late, and a moment later he went smashing into the wall.

He yelped and bounced back, clutching his knee. One of the other White team members, their captain probably, started waving her arms at one hex of the sphere, which abruptly went clear and emitted the referee, an older woman in the traditional pure white.

The ref's whistle went, and play stopped. The sparetime clock started running in big glowing yellow digits that hung in the air in the middle of the sphere. "Injury check," said the ref over the annunciator, "San Diego, Sanderson, number eight . . ."

Sanderson hung there curled up like a poked caterpillar, gasping for breath. Muttering and the occasional sarcastic shout of "Aww!" came from the crowd, some of whom were plainly not convinced of how real the injury was . . . and they had reason, considering the venue in which this game was being played. But the ref soared over to Sanderson, kicked just hard enough off the wall to stop herself, and braced herself against the man. The two of them floated a little farther away from the wall with spare inertia. After a moment spent studying the hand interface she pulled out of her back pocket, and checking with the computer that monitored the vectors and forces expended against the wall, the ref said into the annunciator system, "Verified simulated injury, class-two fracture—"

A great moan of annoyance went up from about a third of the spectators. "Player withdrawn," said the ref, "Sanderson, number eight. San Diego has fallen below six men and has no replacements left. San Diego is eliminated."

The groaning turned into active booing as the remaining San Diego team members, their faces now twisted with anger or disappointment, spreadeagled or cannon-balled themselves at the walls, to adhere, not to bounce, and made their way out of the access hex into the free space outside the sphere. "Resume play," said the ref, taking herself out through the ref-hex again, and the count-up clock froze at 00:18:33, then zipped away and minimized itself into one of the display hexes scattered around the circumference of the sphere.

"*Now* we're in for it," Hal said, squirming a little in his seat. "Two-team game . . ."

Catie nodded, watching intently. In the regular season, play stopped and the game went by automatic forfeit to the highest-scoring team of the three when any one team dropped below minimum permitted strength, but this (as Hal had been crowing for the better part of a week) was no longer the regular season. This was the "shoulder season" during which weaker teams got shouldered out, and the number of stronger ones slowly started to reduce, preparing for the "high season" when only the best ones would be left. Looking into the sphere now, though, Catie began to suspect that she was presently looking at at least one of the best ones—and she started to see why her brother had been getting so excited about it lately.

In a flicker the goals had rearranged themselves into two-team configuration, one at each end, but even as they were reassigned to new hexes, they changed once more, mimicking the rotation of the volume as it would have shifted were this game actually being played in an orbital facility of the classic type. The computer managing the space snagged the virtual ball and slung it back into play along the same vector it had been following when the injury clock started running.

Green and Yellow players flung themselves at it from all sides, some impacting again into a central scrum, some jockeying around the sides of this for position, estimating or guessing where the ball would come out when the forces presently slamming into it from all sides finished their initial impacts. From outside the transparent sphere, cries of "Go, Slugs! Go, Slugs!" were getting deafening.

Can't see a thing, Catie thought. *Let's try something different—*

She clenched her jaw slightly and brought up the implant's "heads-up display" for this environment, let the DISPLAY/EXPERIENCE menu scroll down past her eyes, and blinked at the choice that read PLAYER. A secondary menu now seemed to hang in the air in front of her, listing all the remaining players. Her eyes lit on the name at the top of the list, BRICKNER. She blinked at it—

—and suddenly Catie was in the middle of that scrum, and she was sweating like a pig, and someone was elbowing her hard in the ribs and someone else's feet were pushing down on her head, and the whole world seemed to be made up of arms and legs and torsos straining against one another, like something out of one of Michelangelo's nightmares. But she saw the opening in the tangled sculpture of flesh, the hands of someone else in her colors who had the ball; and she could see what they couldn't, the opening that could be exploited to get it out of there. Two of the players who had been heading in the general direction of the Green goal were still outside this tight-packed pile of people, and she saw a flash of yellow go by outside, in the free space—

Her knee came up. Someone said "Oof!"—and in the slightly larger space made by that person's body contracting, she fisted the ball down out of the hands of the White mid-forward who'd been clutching it, caught it from underneath, and with the leg she'd used to knee the other player, she down-footed the ball, stomping it out that little window of daylight and toward the flash of yellow that had gone by.

Catie swallowed with the other's strain as the pressure of the people got fiercer all around him—and then the nature of the pressure changed, as everybody pushed off as hard as they could, trying to make use of the group's mass and inertia for a good push before the group fragmented and became of less use for this purpose. Daylight opened up all around, but Brickner had eyes for only one piece of it, the piece where the ball had gone, and as the press lessened up around him and the other team went after the ball, his eyes tracked and caught on one particular figure, a slender little woman in yellow who caught the ball in an elbow-bend and flung it away—

Catie felt him swallow. *Bad move*, she started to think, for she couldn't see anyone there to receive. But then another yellow T-shirt flashed in from the side, someone who had managed to get right out to an in-bounds part of the sphere and get a real good push, and the husky young guy hit the ball at full stretch with paired fists, a Superman strike, and yet managed to put enough spin on it so that it missed the White semiforward who was lunging for it. The lunge was a bad one, one of those I-remember-gravity moves that probably hit all but the most experienced spatball players every now and then—the sure sign of a body forgetting for a moment what was going on, and expecting mass to behave as if it were still in a one-gee field instead of microgravity. Beyond that semiforward, one of the other Yellow team members, a little broad-shouldered guy with a brushcut and a feral grin, was ready and waiting. The ball ricocheted off a knee that he seemed just to have left casually waiting there, except for the brutal force he put behind the knee-strike, enough to spin him where he hung. A second later the ball flew like a bullet at the illuminated White goal hex—

A shade too late. The goals precessed again, relocating themselves two hexes along. But Catie gasped as that ball flew straight at her, at the player whose experience she was sharing, and he hit it with his head, twisting his head as he did it, she could feel the muscles strain and feel the cramp hit him a second later, but he whipped his head around nonetheless to see the ball go straight across the sphere, through miraculously empty air, right toward the new location of the White goal, and hit it well inside the boundaries—

The roar of delight and triumph was deafening. The roar of blood in Brickner's ears just about drowned it out, though, as the computer snagged the ball again and fired it back into the sphere's inner volume from just outside the "scoring skin." Catie gasped, trying to sort her own breathing out from his, as the score went to 4–3–3 in South Florida's favor, and things started to get really frantic—for now the crowd had begun to count down the last minute of play.

Mostly when you were "riding" a player virtually via feedback from their implant, in this sport or any other, just about the only thing you couldn't tell for sure was what the players were thinking. But sometimes you didn't have to. Running in full virtual, you could see what they saw—especially one another's eyes—and the opponents' thought processes, at least, showed all too clearly. Every white-uniformed person that Catie saw, in the moments that followed, as the seconds slipped past, had a face which was wearing a terrible expression, a look that said, "I don't believe it! We're going to lose! *I don't believe it*—" But disbelief alone wasn't enough to help them. Play went on, and the White team regained possession and attacked the Yellow goal; but there was a scattered quality to the play, the forward lost the ball to a Yellow half-forward who came arrowing in on an unexpected vector and snagged it out of the air in mid-pass, between her feet.

The White team started to lose it after that. Some of them were already foundering in their own anger or astonishment, literally forgetting what to do with themselves. In spatball, reflexes are everything, and once a player is distracted, it can take time to get them back, but time was what there was less and less of, now, as the unforgiving minute became the unforgiving half-minute, as the truth sank in that there was no way to catch up, no way at all.

And all their captain's shouting at them could only reinforce what was happening, what should have been impossible and was happening anyway. They were going to lose—

"Nineteen!" Catie shouted, in time with a lot of the people in the "stands" around her, though her brother kept still and quiet, and just watched and watched, his attention absolutely riveted on the in-sphere volume. "Eighteen! Seventeen! Sixteen!" The crowd was roaring now, those of them who were in "empathy" with Brickner, seeing what he saw, feeling the abrupt adrenalin flush as he did, a physical thing, a sudden wave of fire in the lower back, the body echoing the mind's realization, *This is it!!* The White team was coming at him all at once, a desperation move, crude at best, though possibly effective enough if it reached him in time, before he had time to act.

The half-forward threw herself into a spin, shot the ball at him like an arrow from a crossbow. And a second later Brickner felt the other push in his back, one of his teammates impacting him at exactly the right moment, offering him for that split second before they "bounced" an opposing force to push against. Brickner rolled backward hard against his buddy's back, kneed the ball as it came to him. It flew again at the White goal—

One of the White players rocketed toward the ball in stretched-out, linear configuration, trying to get there in time, but he didn't have enough inertia to reach it, not having been able to push off soon enough, and his progress slowed, slowed more, he was going to come up short—

The orange ball slammed into the white-lit hex, and the score froze it, half-illuminated, in the very act of precessing.

The roars were making it impossible to hear anything, and when the ball impacted just inside the goal hex, there was no hearing even the usual earsplitting hoot of the scoring alert. It seemed only a few seconds more before the injury-time clock expired, and there was another howl of alarm meant to signify the end of the game, but it was completely lost in the collective howl of the crowd, frustration on two sides, absolute triumph in the third. Suddenly the volume was occupied by a scrum of another kind, one in which George Brickner was completely buried, and deafened by his own hollers of delight and those of his teammates. The world dissolved in yellow.

Catie took a deep breath and brought the menu back, selecting GENERAL and ANNOUNCER. The familiar dulcet voice of the Flyers' home-game announcer was saying, ". . . astonishing comeback from three hexes down, just one more in a series of hairsbreadth saves for South Florida Spat, but a sad moment for San Diego fans, and also for the Seattle High Flyers, after a season that began with such promise but seemed to go rapidly downhill due to injuries and player-contract issues. Again the score, the San Diego Pumas three, the Seattle High Flyers three, and the new interregional title six champions, the South Florida Spatball Association, the 'Banana Slugs,' five—"

Catie blinked to kill her implant. Everything went white, but before she was allowed to shut the feed down completely, a sweet female voice said, "The preceeding expericast is copyright 2025 by the World Spatball Federation. All rights reserved. Any reexperience, pipelining, or other use of this material is restricted to personal use only by international law, and unauthorized transfer of content is strictly prohibited. This is the WSF Net."

The whiteness went away, leaving Catie looking at the far wall of the family room—the bookshelves, her dad's easy chair, the Net computer in its low case, and the place over to one side of the last bookshelf to the right, near the corner of the room, where a crack running down from the ceiling had become apparent in the plaster last week. Her mom had been complaining about the increase in heavy traffic down the street that ran parallel to theirs. It seemed there might be something in what she'd been saying.

"Time?" she said to the clock on the wall.

"Eight fourteen P.M."

"Oh, good," Catie said, glancing out the window at the backyard. The sun was nearly down behind the fruit trees that mostly hid the back wall. Dimming yellow light danced and glittered through their leaves. It had been a nice day, but she hadn't done what she'd first been tempted to, go out and have a few goals with her "casual" soccer team. Instead she had elected to stay home and get the homework done, so that she would have tomorrow and Sunday free. And then Hal had shanghaied her into watching "The Game" with him. *The best-laid plans . . . Oh, well.*

She got out of the implant chair and stretched, and was grateful she didn't have the muscle strain right now that poor Brickner did. If he was smart, his team trainer was putting him into a hot whirlpool bath right about now. Catie stretched again, trying to get rid of a crick in her back that wasn't really there, and glanced around. She had promised her mom that she'd clean up a little in here this evening, but Hal had sidetracked her into watching this game, and now the serious cleaning was going to have to wait until considerably later. *For which I will probably catch a certain amount of grief. Oh, well . . .*

Catie sighed and spent a minute or so moving around the family room, making a desultory attempt to pick up some of the books and magazines and dataflips that had been left lying around. When her little brother caught an interest, he caught it completely. He ate and slept and breathed it . . . until something more interesting came along. Right now it was spatball, and his enthusiasm had been sufficiently contagious, today, to pull her in, too.

For her own part, Catie had to admit that there was something there worth being interested in. Her own acquaintance with the game had been strictly theoretical until the last couple of weeks. Now she knew more about it than she had ever really intended to. And yet at the same time, there was no pretending that the sport wasn't intriguing. Hybrid descendant of soccer in a spacesuit it might be, but—

"Wow, huh?"

The non sequitur had come from Hal, who was standing there now in the doorway of the family room. He apparently hadn't bothered with the postgame show. He was breathing hard, too, which hardly came as a surprise to Catie.

"Wow, yeah," she said. "I didn't think they were going to make it."

"Yeah, it was intense. But the Slugs are go for the eighth-finals!"

Catie chuckled as she watched him wipe the sweat off his forehead. "Were you 'being' George Brickner, too?"

"Who else?"

"There were five other people. That cute brunette you were blathering about last week, for example."

"Oh, her." The tone of voice was dismissive. "Daystrom. She's okay, but she's not as sharp as Brickner is. . . ."

Catie raised her eyebrows at that. "A captain can't be a team all by himself," she said. "Isn't that what you were saying the other day?" She grinned at him as she slipped past him, dropping into his hands some of the books and flips she had been picking up, the ones that were his. "I think it's just a case of hero worship."

"Not a chance!"

She went out into the hall and glanced up and down. "Mom get back from the mall yet?"

"If she did, I didn't hear her."

"I don't think either of us would have heard much if she came in during the last few minutes of that," Catie said, "whether she used the 'outside-in' circuit or not. That crowd was pretty worked up. Where's Dad?"

"No idea."

"Mmf. Probably in the studio."

"Better leave him alone, then."

"Absolutely."

Catie made her way down to the kitchen. It was small for the house, but then, compared to the other houses in their little suburb of D.C., the whole house was small. This was something which Catie's father had of late been complaining about more or less continually. He worked at home, and had been muttering about building another extension onto the house for the past year or so, since he had extended his studio two years ago and then found that what seemed like ample square footage on the plans had turned out too small. Catie turned on the cold water in the sink and let it run for a while, looking around her and wondering how they would all cope when the renovations finally started and left them with no back to the house for a couple of weeks (an image which her mother had been repeatedly invoking in an attempt to get the project put off for a few more months).

She got a tumbler down out of the cabinet and filled it, and drank thirstily. Even though Catie hadn't actually been playing, the mind was still able to fool the body into feeling thirsty sometimes . . . and this was one of those times. Hal came in from the hall and got himself a glass, too, filled it. "He's in the studio," Hal said. "I can hear him scraping on the canvas." Their father was a professional artist, and a quirky one—as talented with old-fashioned media, like paint, as he was with computer-"generated" art and Net-based installations, and sometimes showing what seemed an odd preference for the more archaic media simply on account of their age.

"Right," Catie said. Her dad hadn't been in there yet when she came home, which meant he was good for at least a few hours in there now. She would have time to get a little more of the cleaning-up done before her mom got back and before she had to "go out" herself.

"So let me get this straight," she said, leaning back against the sink and looking out the window of the kitchen at the backyard again. The sun had now gone down behind the wall. "Brickner is the friend you've been telling me about? 'The Parrot'?"

"No, Mike's the friend—I met him on that research project for school last year, the geology thing—he was a research assistant at the Smithsonian for the summer. The Parrot is *Mike's* friend; they know each other from college. I haven't actually met George yet, but Mike says he's going to get us together sometime in the next couple of weeks, if they have the time."

"From the sound of it, I wouldn't be surprised if that team doesn't have much time for casual meetings in the next couple of weeks," Catie said, eyeing her brother.

"They're going to have the media all over them, I bet. They're pretty hot. They play like, I don't know, like a bunch of astronauts."

Hal laughed. "Yeah, they do. . . . Though I bet if the astronauts had known what kind of salary people would start making from this kind of thing, ten years ago, they all would have quit NASA and gone right into the majors."

"The majors don't seem to be the only way to go," Catie said, "if your pet team is anything to go by."

"No," Hal said, "they're kind of a special case."

Catie laughed. "With a name like The Banana Slugs, I guess they'd have to be."

Her brother gave her a look. "It's just a nickname. Anyway, it's not half as stupid as some of the team names these days."

He had a point there. "Still," Catie said, "they're really good. Better than I thought they would be."

"Why shouldn't they be?" Hal said, getting himself another glass of water, and pausing to drink it right down. "It's not like this is a game where you have to have a lot of money to be good at it, or have corporate sponsorship patches plastered all over you. Skill and speed and brains are everything. Doesn't matter whether you're big or small. If you're quick and smart, and fairly well coordinated . . . that should be enough. But there's more to it than just that."

"A certain elegance of execution," Catie said. "One that looks like telepathy sometimes."

Her brother looked at her with some surprise.

"Didn't think I could appreciate the higher aspects of the game?" Catie said mildly. "Well, that's okay. It's healthy for you to underestimate me."

He poked her in the ribs . . . or started to. Abruptly Catie wasn't there anymore, having neatly sidestepped him as soon as he moved. A moment later she was sitting at the kitchen table, giving him an amused look. Her own skill at soccer had not left her entirely without abilities useful for dealing with a rogue brother. . . . Not that Hal needed a lot of dealing with, thank heaven. Their relationship was amiable enough, generally. And the resemblance between them was strong. They could have been twins. They *should* have been twins, Catie sometimes thought, except that Hal was always late, and had apparently managed this stunt even as regarded his birth, turning up a year after a proper twin would have. Regardless of the delay, Hal had come out about the same height as Catie, about the same weight, blonde and blue-eyed like her; and their general build and carriage were like enough that sometimes people mistook them for one another from a distance, especially in the winter when they were bundled up. This could have been a pain, except that Catie was continually amused at being mistakenly hailed as "Hallie" by her brother's would-be girlfriends . . . and it gave Catie endless ammunition to use on him later, while doing her best to make sure that he never had the chance to do the same to her. The situation was entirely satisfactory, as far as she was concerned.

"How am I supposed to discipline you if you won't stand still?" Hal said, getting one more glass of water.

"You're not," Catie said. "Learn to live with your sorry fate and like it."

Her brother made a face eloquent of his opinion of such a philosophy. "You should see yourself," Catie said. "If only you could get stuck that way, Dad could frame you and hang you as a fake Picasso."

"Yeah, right. So, do you want to come watch the postgame show?"

"Can't," Catie said. "Got a Net Force Explorers meeting tonight."

Her brother looked at her incredulously. "You sure that's more important?"

"Yeah. And isn't the postgame show on right now, anyway?"

Hal rolled his eyes. "What planet have you been living on? We get twenty minutes of commercials first. But they're interviewing Brickner. I thought you'd want to see that."

That made Catie pause for a moment. Insight into another athlete's head was always welcome, especially after a game like that. But after a second's thought she shook her head. "Naah," Catie said. "Look, save it for me, okay? Just read it over to my Net space when you're done."

"I can't get into your space."

She smiled sweetly. "Which just proves you've been trying to again. Without asking."

Hal gave her a rather cheesy but completely unrepentant grin.

"One of these days," Catie said, "you're gonna do something on the up-and-up and then be shocked to find that it worked better than making convoluted plans and plots and sneaking around." Then Catie grinned. "But when that happens I'll probably expire of shock, so don't rush, okay? Just ask the space to let you in . . . it'll make an exception for once."

"Okay."

He sounded unusually meek. Catie started wondering what he was up to. She went over to the sink, rinsed her glass out, and opened the dishwasher.

"I'm clean! I'm clean!" the dishwasher shrilled.

"That's more than *I* can say," Catie muttered, realizing afresh how sweaty even a virtual game of spatball had left her. Her T-shirt was sticking to her. She shut the dishwasher and put the glass aside on the counter. "I thought you were supposed to empty this thing all this week."

"I was busy—"

"Get on with it," Catie said. "If you hurry, I won't have to tell Mom about it when she gets back."

"And if you hurry, *I* won't have to tell her you didn't clean up the family room."

Catie rolled her eyes. "Blackmail," she said. "Empty threats. I need a shower. And then I'm going to go do adult things."

"I'll get you your cane, O superannuated one."

Catie smiled a crooked smile and went out, rubbing her neck, then caught herself massaging the sports injury she didn't have, and smiled more crookedly still as she went down the hall to the bathroom.

Somewhere else entirely a meeting was taking place in a bar. It was a virtual bar, and the drink was virtual, and the customers were all wearing seemings, which well suited their purpose, in most cases, since most of them were intent on keeping their business to themselves.

Under a ceiling of blue glass, a tall, blunt-featured man with hair cut very, very short was sitting at one of the tables nearest the big central fountain, a bowl of tan, blue-veined marble. The man was dressed in an ultrablack single-all of extremely conservative cut, with a white silk jabot at the throat, and he was turning a martini glass around and around on the matte white marble of the ta-bletop. His face was very still, giving no indication of the turmoil of thought presently going on inside it. His mouth twitched once or twice, an expression that could have been taken for a smile, but that impression would have been very incorrect.

Outside the bar it was afternoon, or pretending to be. The light lay long and low and golden over the pedestri-anized street outside, as people strolled up and down it with shopping bags and small children in tow. Something came between the afternoon light pouring through the windows and the man sitting by the fountain, blocking away the golden glint of the afternoon light on the martini glass. The man in the ultrablack single-all looked up and squinted slightly at the second man standing there.

The newcomer sat down casually enough in the other chair. The first man looked at him for a few moments. The second man was small, broad-shouldered but thick around the waist, and dressed in slikjeans and a dark blazer with a white T-shirt underneath, a look that sug-gested the wearer was caught among several different eras and trying to fulfil fashion imperatives from all of them. *Scattered*, thought the first man. *Don't know why I'm bothering—*

"Thanks for coming, Darjan," said the second man, and looked the first one casually in the face, then glanced away again.

"Don't thank me, Heming," said Darjan. "We have a problem."

"Yeah, I heard the results," Heming said.

"A big problem," said Darjan. "We started hearing from

the syndicate's backers within about ten minutes of the win."

"They're just nervous, I can understand wh—"

"You can't understand what *they* understand," Darjan said, "which is that the pools projections never indicated anything like this happening, and a lot of people are going to be out a lot of money unless something's done."

"It's luck," said Heming, shrugging. "The kind of thing you can't predict."

Darjan laughed harshly. "With the computers you people have, with probability experts who can even get the *weather* right, nowadays, five days out of six, you're telling me this kind of 'luck' couldn't be predicted? You people were so sure that your prognostication algorithms were foolproof. Well, we're about to be the fools. And the booby prize has more zeroes after it than you're ever going to want to see. Something has to be done!"

"Look," said Heming, starting to look alarmed for the first time, "it really is just a run of luck. It can't last. If they—"

"You're damned right it isn't going to last," said Darjan, going suddenly grim. "Accidents are going to start happening. Their luck's run out."

Heming looked more nervous still. "Listen," he said. "There are ways . . . You wouldn't want to ruin everything by getting too . . . you know . . . overt. If someone should suspect—"

"Suspicion we can live with," said Darjan, pushing the martini glass away from him in disgust. "Losing one point five billion dollars or so, that we can't live with for a second . . . and no one else is going to be allowed to live with it, either."

"One point five . . ."

"That was the last estimate." Darjan looked up from under those thick dark brows at Heming. "What the hell are those people doing *playing* at this level? They're a local team, for God's sake. They're a bunch of housewives and appliance repairmen; they're the damned *Kiwanis*!"

"They're good," said Heming, rather helplessly.

"They're *too* good," Darjan said, frowning. "And something's gonna be done about it, one way or another. Too much rides on things going the way they were planned to go at the beginning of the season. The spreads, even the *casual* betting spreads, are going to be disturbed. We can't have it, Heming. The investors are going to turn their backs on us, and some of them we spent too much time and money getting hold of in the first place to lose now. So you better tell me what you have in mind . . . otherwise 'overt' is going to be the order of the day, whether you like it or not."

Heming shook his head. "You wouldn't want to—"

"Don't tell me what I want. Instead tell me how you're going to fix it. Nonovertly."

Heming thought for a moment. "Well, some of it would be an outgrowth of how we would keep things running normally outside of the playoffs."

Darjan considered this for a moment. "You're going to have to 'oil' different people," he said. "Higher up. The kind who'd be more likely to blow the whistle."

"Not if the incentives are correctly applied," said Heming, "and if they're big enough. Everybody has their price. Just a matter of seeing how high you have to go. . . . And after that, because of the increased price . . . they're that much more eager to keep quiet. Because if word ever gets out . . ." He smiled. "Scandal. Bad publicity. Lawsuits, public prosecutions, jail terms . . . All very messy."

"And you can hold that over them, of course."

"Of course. The leaks would seem to come from somewhere else, somewhere 'respectable,' when they came."

The first man nodded slowly. "All right. We can try it your way first. Do you have some targets in mind?"

"Several."

"Get on it, then. Do what you have to. But hurry up! This was the last of the preliminary bouts. The serious betting always starts at the eighth-final level. It's started already. The whole structure of the 'pools' betting will start to be affected soon, if you don't get them out of the running."

Heming looked thoughtful for a moment. "Obviously

we won't get results until the first eighth-final game," he said.

"That's Monday," Darjan said. "South Florida versus Chicago versus Toronto, if I remember correctly. Chicago was scheduled to win, when the third was going to be New Orleans." His face set grim, and he glanced up. "Certain people," he said, "were—*are*—very committed to Chicago. Believe me, you wouldn't like to have to explain to them how their team got knocked out at the eighth-final stage by a bunch of landscape gardeners and sanitation engineers. *Amateurs*—"

"It won't happen," said Heming.

"Pray that it doesn't," said Darjan. "Get on it. Get in touch with me tomorrow and tell me what progress you've made."

Heming went out hurriedly through the open French doors to the square, where the afternoon light was beginning to tarnish. Darjan looked after him, once more reaching around to the martini glass and beginning to turn it around and around on the white marble. Then his hand clenched slowly around the stem. A moment later there was a sharp *crack* as the stem of the Dartington crystal, tough as it was, gave way. This being virtual experience, there was no blood.

Elsewhere, however, Darjan thought, *in reality, unless Heming gets busy, things will be very different. . . .*

2

The monthly regional Net Force Explorers meetings could turn into a real mob scene sometimes, so Catie liked to get to them early when she could. But that evening she was almost foiled in this intention by her mother, who, just as Catie was heading back down to the family room, came edging in through the kicked-open front door with her arms full of shopping bags, and also with several canvas bags full of books hanging from her, so that she looked like some very overworked beast of burden. "Oh, honey, help!" her mom said. "The groceries—!"

Catie hurried down the front hall to her and did her best to relieve her mom of the two heaviest bags, which were just about to fall out of her mother's arms. "Mom, why can't you leave stuff in the car and just make another trip?"

"I thought I could manage it," her mother gasped as they staggered together into the kitchen and dumped everything on the table. Catie shook her head as they straightened up and dusted themselves off. "Supermom," Catie said in a chiding tone.

"Oh, sweetie, I just hate making two trips, you know how it is. . . ."

"Inefficient," they said in unison. Catie smiled a slightly rueful smile. Her mother worked at the Library of Congress as an acquisitions librarian, and had spent the first two years of her employment trying to work a reorganization of the basic stacks system through the library's monolithic bureaucracy. Now, six years later, having been promoted to senior acquisitions librarian in charge of classical literature, she was still at it—for while efficiency was not precisely one of Colleen Murray's gods, it was at least a minor idol before which she bowed at regular intervals, in the name of making the world in general work better. This being the case, Catie knew she was something of a cross for her mother to bear, for Catie felt in her soul that it was wrong to have a house, or a life, look from minute to minute as if you were expecting to have *Architectural Digest* come in to do a photo shoot. A little randomness around the edges, a little easygoing clutter here and there, in Catie's opinion, made things look less artificial, more natural and human. *And since they get that way anyhow, in the normal course of things, your nerves don't get shredded trying to prevent the unavoidable. . . .*

Now the table looked more than random enough even for Catie. Books and foodstuffs shared it about evenly, and Catie started divvying them up, paying more attention to the books, with an eye to keeping them safely away from the food. The first few volumes she picked up seemed to be printed in Greek, and another was in a lettering she didn't recognize. "What's *this*?" she said. Its title seemed to say RhOIQEA AFOI-ITUW, except that some of the letters looked wrong: the *L* was backward, the *F* had an extra stroke underneath the short one, and the *h* was hitched up between the *P* and *O* like some kind of punctuation mark with delusions of letterhood.

Catie's mother was loading a couple of gallons of milk into the fridge. She paused to peer around the door. "Oh. That's the King James Bible translated into Tataviam."

Catie gave her a look. "Didn't know you were into science fiction, Mom. Which series are the Tataviam from? Galactic Patrol?"

Her mother laughed as she shut the refrigerator door. "It's not a created language, honey. It's native to the Los Angeles area. The Native Americans there had about a hundred languages and dialects. Highest density of languages per square mile in the world, supposedly."

Catie shook her head and put the book down. She had been about to ask her mother why she'd brought this particular book home, but it occurred to her that listening to the whole answer would probably wind up making her late. Her mom picked up a pile of cans of beans and vegetables from the table, stacking them up carefully in her arms, and took them over to unload them into one of the undercounter cabinets, while Catie went through the other books—mostly works of Greek and Latin classicists like Pliny and Strabo and Martial.

Her mother meanwhile finished with the cans, got herself a glass of water, drank it in a few gulps, and pulled the dishwasher door open. "I'm *empty*!" said the dishwasher in a tone of ill-disguised triumph.

"Isn't that super," Catie's mother said, putting the glass in and closing the dishwasher again. "Your brother's finally beginning to get the idea. Perhaps my life has not been in vain."

Catie smiled gently and said nothing. "Mom," she said, "anything important you need to tell me before I make myself socially unavailable?"

Her mother looked thoughtful. "Nothing leaps right out at me. What is it tonight? Net Force Explorers meeting?"

"Yeah."

"Have fun. I'll take care of the rest of this." Catie smiled again, a little more broadly. She knew her mother preferred to take care of the groceries herself, so that she wouldn't have to accuse her daughter of "misshelving." "Where's your dad?"

"Incommunicado. In the studio."

"Painting?"

"That, or plastering," Catie said. "Hal reported faint scraping noises. But it's probably just painting, since I forgot the spackle on the way home, and so did Hal."

Her mother sighed. "Okay. Where's Hal taken himself, by the way?"

"He may still be on the Net with his post-spatball game show. I didn't check."

"Fine. You go do your thing, Catie. I have to look these over and see if we need to order copies for the department."

"Mom, they shouldn't make you take your work home," Catie said, frowning.

Her mother chortled at her. "Honey, it's not that they make me, it's that they can't *stop* me. You know that. Go on, get out of my hair."

Catie went down to the family room and shut the door, then settled into the implant chair again, lined up her implant with it, and clenched her jaw to activate it.

Instantly the room vanished, and Catie was sitting in an identical chair surrounded by the spectacular polished pillars, shining staircases, murals and mosaics which filled the gold-brown-and-white "front hall" of the Library of Congress. Her mother used a similar entry to her workspace, as a lot of her colleagues did. They felt a natural pride in having as part of their "turf" one of the most spectacular and ornate buildings in the entire Capitol District, a gem of the Beaux-Arts tradition, more like a palace than a library. Catie, though, simply liked the palatial aspect of it, and the sense of everything in it having been made by people's hands, not by fabricating machines or computer programs.

She got out of the chair and started up the grand staircase to the gallery that overlooked the main reading room. "Hey, Space!" Catie said as she climbed.

"Good evening, Catie," said her workspace in a cultured male voice.

"Any mail for me?"

"Nothing since you last checked in."

"Nothing? In three whole hours?" That was mildly unusual.

"Would I lie to you?"

"Not if you wanted to keep your job," Catie said, while knowing perfectly well that her workspace management program was about as likely to lie to her as her brother was to unload the dishwasher without being reminded.

"I live in fear of firing," the management program said, dry-voiced.

Catie raised an eyebrow. She had asked one of her Net Force buddies to tinker with the program's responsiveness modes some weeks back, and very slowly since then she had started to notice that it was developing what appeared to be a distinct strain of sarcasm. "Good," she said as she came to the top of the stairs, "you do that."

At the head of the stairs she stood in the big doorway there and looked through it and down. At this spot, in the real library, there was a gallery along the back wall of the main reading room, with a glass baffle to keep the readers from being disturbed by the sound of the never-ending stream of tourists. But in Catie's version of the library there was no glass, only a doorway leading down into whatever other virtual space she should elect to visit. For the moment the door was filled with a swirling, glowing opalescent smoke effect, something Catie had designed for her mother as a "visual soother," a distraction pattern for when she had to put someone on hold at the office.

"What's your pleasure?" the management program said to her.

"Net Force Explorers meeting," Catie said. "The usual address."

"Net Force," said her management program, and the smoke began to clear away. "I don't think they suspect anything yet, so don't blow it."

I definitely need to talk to the guilty party about this, Catie thought. She stepped through the doorway, pausing on the landing of another stairway which formed to let her down into the big, echoing, empty space on the other side.

It wasn't precisely empty. There were probably about fifty other kids there already, milling around and chatting, while above them hung suspended in space, glowing, a giant Net Force logo. It was ostensibly just as a courtesy that Net Force had set aside virtual "meeting space" on its own servers for these meetings. But Catie sometimes wondered whether there was some more clandestine agenda involved, some obscure security issue . . . or just a desire to "keep an eye on the kids." For her own part, she didn't much mind. *There's always the possibility that there are some of the "grown-ups" in here strolling around in disguise, listening to the conversations of the junior auxiliary and noting down which of us seem promising. . . .* A moment later Catie put the thought aside as slightly paranoid. Yet, thinking about it, she decided it wouldn't particularly bother her if that *were* happening. Catie firmly intended to wind up working for Net Force one day, doing image processing and analysis, or visuals-management work of one kind or another. If the cutting edge, in terms of excellence, opportunity, and potential excitement, was to be found anywhere, it was there. If someone from the adult side of Net Force wanted to look her over with that sort of work in mind, it was fine by her. *The sooner the better, in fact. . . .*

Meanwhile, she had other fish to fry. Or one fish, a small one. As she came down the stairs to floor level, she paused, glancing over the group beneath her. A few faces she knew, a lot she didn't, not that *that* had ever bothered her. She always left one of these meetings with at the very least a bunch of new acquaintances—

And there was the one she wanted to see. She finished coming down the stairs and walked around the edges of the small crowd, greeting a couple of people she knew as she passed—Megan O'Malley, Charlie Davis—and then walked over to her target from behind quietly, with the air of someone approaching a small and possibly danger-ous animal without wanting to unduly frighten it.

"Hey, there, Squirt!" Catie said with an edge to her voice.

The figure actually jumped a little, and turned. A slight young boy, young especially when you considered that a lot of the other kids here were older by at least several years, tending toward their late teens. But Mark Gridley was no more than thirteen: dark-haired, dark-eyed, with Thai in his background and the devil in his eyes. "Ah," Mark said. "Ah, Catie, hi, how are you . . ."

"You're here early," Catie said.

"Slumming," Mark said idly.

"*Oh*, yeah," Catie said. Since she'd first met him at one of these meetings, she'd been aware that Mark was obsessed with the idea that somehow, somewhere, he might possibly be missing out on something interesting. Even being the son of Net Force's director was just barely enough "interesting" to keep him going, so that Mark routinely went looking for more. He was always early to these meetings, though he went out of his way to make it look accidental.

"How's the artwork doing?" Mark said, with the air of someone who wanted to distract her from something. "Still fingerpainting?"

Catie grinned a little, and flexed those fingers. "Hey, everybody in the plastic arts has to start somewhere," she said. "It's what you do with the medium, anyway, not what everybody else does with it. Besides, it never keeps me away from the image work long." She knew perfectly well that Mark knew this was her forte. There were few Net-based effects, in the strictly visual and graphical sense, that Catie couldn't pull off with time and care. No harm in him knowing, either. Who knew, he might mention it to his father, and his father might mention it to James Winters, the Net Force Explorers liaison, and after that anything might happen. *Networking is everything,* Catie thought. "And how about you?" she said then. "The French police give up on you finally?"

Mark scowled, and blushed. He had gotten in some slight trouble recently when traveling with his dad, and those of the Net Force Explorers who knew the details were still teasing Mark about the episode, half out of envy that Mark had time to get in trouble while staying somewhere as interesting as Paris, and half out of the sheer amusement of watching him squirm—for Mark was hypercompetent on the Net and hated to come out on the wrong side of anything. "It wasn't a big deal," he said. "But enough about my scrapes. *You're* the one who's always getting yourself scraped up." He tilted his head back and pretended to be peering at Catie's elbows and knees.

She laughed at him. Catie had long been used to this kind of comment from her friends, both those at school and even those who were also Net Force Explorers. She had been in soccer leagues of one kind or another almost since she was old enough to walk, partly because of her dad's interest in the sport, but partly because she liked it herself. Then, later on, as virtual life became more important to her, Catie began to discover its "flip side"— that reality had its own special and inimitable tang which even the utter freedom of virtuality couldn't match. There was no switching off the implant and having everything be unchanged or "all better" afterward. Life was life, irrevocable, and the cuts and bruises you carried home from a soccer game were honestly earned and genuine, yours to keep. Some of her friends thought she was weird to take the "real" sports so seriously, but Catie didn't mind.

"To each his, her, or its own," her father would say, chucking aside some rude review of one of his exhibitions, and picking up the brush again. Catie found this a useful approach with the virtuality snobs, who usually had what passed for their minds made up and tended not to be very open to new data.

"Nope, nothing new to exhibit," Catie said. "Except for a new interest. A slight one, anyway. Spatball."

"Huh," said Mark, glancing around. The space was beginning to fill up fast now, a couple of hundred kids having come in over the space of just the last few minutes. "The last refuge of the space cadet, one of my cousins calls it."

"It might indeed be that," Catie said. "I'm in the process of making up my mind. Meanwhile, Squirt, there's something I've been meaning to talk to you about."

"Yeah?"

"My workspace management program is beginning to sass me."

"Oh?"

Mark looked completely innocent. It was an expression which struck Catie as coming entirely too easily to him. "It's getting positively sarcastic lately," she said. "This wouldn't be anything of *your* doing, would it? Some little bug you slipped in?"

"There are no bugs," Mark said virtuously, "only features."

"Yeah, well, this 'feature' has you written all over it."

He acquired a very small smile. "Just a little heuresis, Cates. It only does what it sees you doing. So if it's getting sarcastic—"

She took a swipe at him, and missed, mostly on purpose. At the same time, Catie had to grin a little. "So the computer's chips are turning into chips off the old block, huh. Cute. One of these days you're going to do something too cute to allow you to live any longer, Squirt."

He gave her a look that suggested he didn't think this was all that likely. *The problem was,* Catie thought, *that he was probably right.* Assuming that he survived through his teens—for Mark's "scrapes" were many and varied, so that Catie thought it was probably miraculous that his parents hadn't simply killed him by now—the talent that got him into the scrapes would eventually take him far. For all his tender years, Mark was a native Net programmer of great skill, one of those people who seem to be born with a logic solid in their mouths and are better at programming languages than spoken ones. There was very little that Mark couldn't make a computer do, and the more complex the computer was, the more likely Mark was to deliver the results. But he would also find a way to enjoy himself in the meantime . . . and his enjoyment could occasionally also mean your annoyance, if you let him get away with it.

Catie gave him a look. "If the management system starts interfering with my space's functioning," she said, "I'm going to debug the software with an ax . . . and then hunt you down and take the lost time out of your hide. Meantime, what's on the agenda tonight? I didn't have time to look at it before I came in."

"Something about a virtual field trip to the new Cray-Nixdorf-Siemens 'server farm' complex in Dusseldorf," Mark said. "They're going to run a lottery to allow some of us in there to have a look at the firmware. Like the

new Thunderbolt warm-superconductor storage system."
He had a slightly hungry gleam in his eye.

Catie nodded. "Sounds like it's right up your alley.
Why should you need to enter a lottery, though? Can't
your dad get you in?"

"Not really," Mark said, sounding disappointed. "The
offer has all the usual 'not for industry associates and their
families' disclaimer all over it. Besides, I've been
busy. . . ."

He trailed off a little too soon. Catie was about to ask
him what was really going on when she was interrupted
by a banging noise coming from the center of the room.
All around her, people were making themselves chairs or
lounges to sit on, and in the middle of things there had
appeared, off to one side, what appeared to be an
Olympic-sized swimming pool. A moment later there also
appeared, under the Net Force logo, something that could
have been mistaken for the great mahogany half-
hexagonal bench in the court chamber of the Supreme
Court . . . except that the center position was occupied
solely by a young slim redheaded guy in process blue
slikshorts and a LightCrawl T-shirt that presently had the
message I'M IN CHARGE HERE, HONEST inching its way
around his chest cavity in flashing red block capitals.

"Can everyone hold it down?" he was yelling. "We
have to get started. . . ."

Catie glanced up. "Who's that?"

"Chair for the meeting, I guess," Mark said.

"I knew that. I meant, 'Do you know him?' "

"Uh, no. Hey, Gwyn . . ."

"Hey," said one of the other kids presently beginning
to drift over to where Mark was standing. Catie looked
them over thoughtfully, for people that Mark didn't mind
hanging around him tended to be worth knowing. Either
he found *them* intelligent, or they were sufficiently capa-
ble of getting far enough past his extreme impulsiveness
and mischievousness to notice that *he* was intelligent. Either of these were characteristics that Catie thought were
likely to be useful at some point. What was also moder-
ately interesting was that the kids gathering around Mark

all looked significantly older than he . . . more Catie's age, in the seventeen- or eighteen-year-old area. Plainly they weren't concerned about the age difference when the younger kid was as smart as Mark. *Or has his connections,* Catie thought. *Networking is everything. . . .*

"Okay," said the kid who had been banging on the mahogany bench, "we have some announcements first—"

"Who are you?" came the predictable yell from the floor, a ragged, amused chorus of about thirty voices. It always seemed to happen, no matter how many times they all met, to the point where it was now approaching tradition: a speaker would be shocked out of composure by the sight of all those faces and forget to introduce himself.

"Oh. Sorry. I'm Neil Linkoping. As I was saying—"

"Hi, Neil," came the cheerfully mocking reply from the floor, about a hundred of them this time. Neil grinned and said, "Hi, crowd. Now, as I was saying . . . we have some announcements first. . . ."

Groans and shouts of "Not again!" ensued. These were traditional, too, because there were *always* announcements. They were about the only thing that could be counted on to happen at every meeting. Neil wisely ignored the noise from the floor and started to read from a transparent window that popped into existence in the air in front of him. Catie could see the text content, in glowing letters, scrolling down through it. Near where Mark was sitting in what appeared to be an Eames chair of venerable lineage, Catie now made herself a copy of her workspace chair, itself a copy of the very beat-up Tattersall-checked "comfy chair" in the corner of her bedroom, and curled up in it to watch the proceedings unfold.

They did so with many halts, pauses, and interruptions—some genial, some adolescently crass, and some simply constituting demands for more information about one topic or another. Neil slogged his way through them, methodically enough, but with good humor, like someone used to interruptions from some other group, possibly a large family. This was the way things normally went at the regional meetings Catie had attended—a progression of events always verging cheerfully on chaos, but never quite tipping over the edge. After the announcements members might take the floor to talk about a Net seminar they were organizing, or something that had come up in a gaming or simming group, or some other issue that they thought would be of interest to the gathered Net Force Explorers as a whole. People popped in and out all during the meeting to suit their own schedules, though there was a long-agreed consensus that they should keep quiet as they did it. No appearing suddenly in bursts of virtual flame or other distracting manifestations. This rule was occasionally broken, but since breaking it infallibly caused the person who'd created the distraction to be chucked into the virtual "pool" and hence out of the meeting, with no chance of return, people tended not to do it more than once. However, even with all the noise, joking, and chaos, there was always an undercurrent of seriousness at these get-togethers. Everyone at them, or nearly everyone, intended to try to get into Net Force eventually, and the intensity of their intention as a group tended to shake out those who weren't serious in pretty short order.

About half an hour went by in this way, and gradually Catie began to realize that nothing being discussed was particularly interesting to her. But there were other matters to think about. Toward the end of another Net Force Explorer's brief presentation about a new virtual "chip-constant" diagnosis routine for house pets, and an upcoming Explorers charity fund-raiser to cover chipping costs for pet owners who found it hard to afford, that particular Explorer—a blond girl of maybe sixteen—finished up with: "And for all of you who made it here late after celebrating this evening's victory by South Florida Spat—"

"*Yayy!*" went a surprising number of voices from the floor, and in the middle of the crowd a small raucous chorus of voices began singing, "What's that slithering sound you hear? / We are the Slugs, and revenge is near—!" In response, "Fly High Seattle!" yelled one lone voice from the back, and was answered with a fair amount of teasing laughter from all over the room.

Catie raised her eyebrows at that, glancing around the

floor. Her gaze suddenly rested on Mark and paused. He had gotten up out of his Eames chair to go have a word with slim, dark, little Charlie Davis, but now Mark was standing near Charlie and looking around the crowd with an unusually thoughtful expression. Seeing that look made Catie start to feel thoughtful herself. You didn't normally see such expressions on Mark Gridley without good reason. *He's up to something,* she thought, knowing that particular focused look too well from her own brother. *Just what* is *he up to?*

Neil Linkoping had gotten up behind the bench again and was once more pounding on it. "Anybody else?" he said. "Going once . . ."

There were already people standing up, already having vanished the chairs they had created for themselves or had arrived in. Catie got up and stretched herself, looking around her. *I might have saved myself the trouble,* she thought. It was the usual thing, though. As summer came on, a lot of the Explorers got more interested in topics that had to do with vacations, or (while the weather cooperated) the Real World. "Going twice?" Neil said.

". . . You going to any more spat games?"

Catie looked around and down. Mark Gridley was standing next to her again.

"Going three times . . ."

Catie did her best to keep her curiosity, now raging, out of her face. "Probably," she said. "It has its points. I'm starting to wonder if it's something I want to play myself. Anyway, my brother wants me to meet a friend of a friend of his who's a professional spat player. I'll probably wind up going to the game before we actually meet."

"Really?" Mark said. "Sounds pretty space. Who is it?"

"Uh, his name is Brickner. George Brickner."

"Sold for a dollar," Neil Linkoping was saying to the meeting at large. "That's it. Meeting's archived. Next meeting is July thirteenth. Night, everybody . . ."

All around them everybody was getting up, but for the moment Catie was ignoring them. Mark was looking thoughtful. "South Florida?"

"That's right. They call him 'The Parrot.' Don't ask me why."

"Really," Mark said. His expression was momentarily distant.

"Yeah," Catie said, watching him curiously.

"Well, maybe I'll run into you during the tournament sometime," Mark said.

That surprised her, too. Catie wouldn't normally have thought that Mark had anything even slightly jockish about him. "Maybe," she said.

"Do me a favor, though?"

"Sure, what?"

"If you do ever meet Brickner, drop me a virtmail and tell me what he's like."

Catie was surprised again. Then she grinned. "Mark, don't tell me you're a secret fan of this guy's. . . ."

Mark's eyes widened slightly. An embarrassed look? Or something less spontaneous? "Okay," Mark said then, "I won't tell you." And he grinned, turned away, and got very obviously interested in something that tall, slim Megan O'Malley, on the other side of him, was saying to a third Net Force Explorer, a short redheaded guy that Catie didn't recognize.

For her own part, Catie moved away a little, too, thinking. *He didn't actually answer my question. . . .*

And that decided her. She was going to go out of her way, now, to make sure that this meeting with her brother's friend's friend would happen . . . and as soon as possible.

Catie waved good night at Maj Green, halfway across the room and talking fast to a handsome dark-haired young guy. *Got to virtmail her about that simming conference. She's been getting into that kind of thing. . . .* Then she re-created the doorway back into her own workspace. She stepped through it and came out in the gallery over the LOC's main reading room. There, musing, Catie paused for a moment, then turned and faced the door again. "Hal's place," she said.

The iridescent blue "hold" pattern swirled in the doorway, but, rather to her surprise, didn't immediately dis-

solve. "Casual visitors are being discouraged," said
Catie's workspace management program.

"Since when am I a 'casual visitor'?" Catie said. "Tell
him it's me."

"No! No! *Nooooo!*" came her brother's voice, followed
by a terrible but (to her ears) rather artificial scream.

"I give it a six," Catie said after a moment. "Hal, I'm
serious, I need to talk to you for a minute."

There was a groan on the other side of the virtual interface. Then the "hold" pattern dissolved, and Catie
stepped through the doorway, glanced around her—and
stood still in surprise.

Normally Hal's workspace looked like a parts warehouse, full of rack storage shelves which in turn were full
of "cardboard boxes," all symbolic containers for his
many files. Catie had spent many hours teasing him about
minimalist retrotech, and what kind of person would take
a workspace which could look like anything possible that
human imagination could devise, and turn it into something like the warehouse end of a catalog store. Now,
though, Catie got the feeling that she was going to be able
to raise the teasing to a whole new level. A circle of high,
gloomy walls built of blocks of splotched gray stone rose
up all around her, and all kinds of bizarre electrical ap-
paratus were lined up against them, buzzing and sparking:
strange rotating wheels spitting blue-fire electrical
discharge, Tesla coils up and down which writhing arcs
of electricity slid and sizzled. As imagery went, it was a
superlative job. Hal had plainly gone to some trouble to
get the proportions right. Even the sound effects were
right on. Catie could hear peasants shouting outside, and
if she stuck her head out one of the high Gothic-arched
windows, she was sure she would see that they had
torches and pitchforks. *This is hysterical*, she thought, *but
I wonder what brought this on. . . .*

"Hal?" she said.

"What is it, Cates? I'm busy." Her brother appeared
from behind a cabinet, carrying an Erlenmeyer flask and
a few glass-stoppered bottles over to a workbench that, to
judge by the stains on it, had seen better days. Hal was

wrapped in a high-collared white lab coat, and except for the bottles, he looked entirely like someone who might start stitching pieces of people together without warning, without much attention being paid to the principle of informed consent.

"This a private project," Catie said, coming down the curved stone stairs around the outside of the tower, "or something for school?"

"Both," he said, putting the flasks down. "You interrupting me just for spiteful personal pleasure, or as a public service?"

"Both," Catie said, giving him a look. "I didn't think you'd be done with the postgame show already. . . ."

"It was shorter than they expected," Hal said, taking the stopper out of one of the bottles and sniffing it. "Which was just as well, since while I was watching I solved a problem that's been bugging me for a while, and now I can get on with this." He put the stopper back into the bottle and paused to make a note on a pad on the table.

Wow, Catie thought, *he really is intense about this, whatever it is*. Her curiosity threatened to get the better of her, but for the moment she put it aside. "Hal," she said to her brother, "look, about Brickner . . ."

He paused and looked up, frowning. "Catie, I hate to say it, but this is one moment when I don't feel like discussing spat."

"All right! Just very quickly . . . do you think you're gonna be able to work something out with your friend?"

Her brother turned his attention back to his work, but he was grinning now. "Had a look at the *People* interview, did you? So did half the girls your age in the country."

Catie made an annoyed face, then realized there wasn't any point in it. Maybe it was for the better if Hal thought she had a crush on this guy. He'd then go out of his way to see that they met, so that he could see Catie gush and then ride her about it later. "Whatever. When can we set it up?"

"Talk to me tomorrow. If I don't get this to work out, my organic chemistry grade is gonna suffer."

Catie became more curious still, for her brother didn't often discuss his schoolwork with her. "What're you doing?"

"Creating life in a test tube, what else? Cates, *pleeeeze ...*"

She contemplated sticking around to tease him a little more, in order to extract some revenge for last Tuesday, when he had been running the same number on her ... she sighed, deciding it wasn't kind to give him trouble, especially when schoolwork was at issue. "Vanishing," she said. And she did.

Catie found herself standing again in the Great Hall of the Library of Congress's Jefferson Building, looking around at the opulent pillars and mosaics, all gleaming softly in some warm afternoon slanting light. "Hey, Space!" she said.

"Listening with bated breath for your lightest word, boss."

Only features, huh, Catie thought as she made her way across the beautiful mosaics and down the hallway that led to the main reading room. *I'm going to find a way to get Mark for this ... eventually.* She came out into that great octagonal space, all lined two stories high with shelves, and glanced around. Her own "workspace" proper was out in the middle of it, where the big circular mahogany-built reference and stacks-access island would be, but here and now the space was empty. "Yeah, well," Catie said, "if you're paying such assiduous attention to me, you broken-down box of spurious instructions, why isn't my chair where it should be?"

"I was cleaning," said her workspace, and her chair appeared in the center of the space. Catie made her way over and flopped down in it, tucking her legs underneath her. "And you really ought to get that thing reupholstered. Look at the fabric!"

"Reupholstered," Catie said in a reflective sort of voice as she sat down and looked up into the overarching golden glow of the main dome with its upward-spiraling square recesses, a glorious restatement of the old dome of the Pantheon in Rome. "Possibly with your hide."

The clear sky showing through at the top of the dome went abruptly cloudy, and lightning flickered in it, intended (Catie thought) as sarcasm. "Oooh, I don't like the sound of that," said her workspace.

"I just bet you don't. Show me that graphic I was working on last night."

"You don't want to see the mail first?" The workspace manager somehow managed to sound injured.

She rolled her eyes. "Oh, all right. Just the icons."

They appeared on the floor all around her, scattered over the mosaics, along with icons of other kinds: three-dimensional representations of books which represented ongoing pieces of research, piles of sketches or canvases each of which "meant" some piece of art Catie was working on, and virtmail messages which presented themselves as piles of paper with sketches of people or things on them in various media. It was a rather involved and untidy filing system, but Catie had no patience with the stylized representations that a lot of the mail-handling softwares offered you, little cubes and rotating spheres and other such Platonic-ideal solids. Catie liked ideas to look like real things, not abstractions, even if the preference did make Hal snicker and call her a Luddite.

She beckoned one of the piles of messages over. It picked itself up off the floor and sailed through the air to land in her lap. Catie picked up the first sheet, glanced at it. It featured a gaudy, much-scrolled engraving, which harked back to the old-fashioned paper money of the mid-twentieth century, and framed inside the scrollwork were the words YOU MAY BE A WINNER!

Catie breathed out patiently and held up the piece of "paper." She wasn't even going to bother telling its content to reveal itself. "This is something else I've been meaning to talk to you about," she said to her workspace, annoyed. "I told you, I don't want to see advertising, no matter how many zeroes it has on it."

There was a silence, the machine "pretending" to think and react to a request which Catie knew it had already successfully processed some hundreds of milliseconds ago—and the pretense somehow made her smile. She had to admit that Mark Gridley was good at producing a program that made you react to it as if it were intelligent, even when it wasn't.

"Couldn't help it that time, boss," the space manager said after a moment. "It camouflaged itself as a message being returned to you after having been sent from here to some other address, then unshelled itself on being admitted, and nuked the shell."

Catie sighed. There was nothing to be done about that tactic. It was an old favorite among the senders of "spam," or unwanted commercial e-mail, and every time the mail-handling programs found a way to prevent a given tactic, the spammers always found some other way to construct a shell that would fool your system into letting their ads and scams through. She held up the piece of "paper." It incinerated itself in her hand in a swirl of blue fire and went to dust. "How many more of those am I going to find in here?" she said.

"Probably about six, boss," said the management program, for once having the good sense to sound chastened.

Catie turned the next couple of "pages" over and immediately found two more ads, one from someone who wanted to sell her carpets. She thought about handing that one on to her mom, then decided against it. There were already too many virtual decorating brochures cluttering up her mother's workspace, along with various partially assembled "try-out" versions of the back of the house, so that her mom's space was beginning to look like a construction site itself at times. Catie skimmed the carpet message out into the air, where it caught fire and rained down in a dust of instantly vanishing ash, to be followed a moment later into bright oblivion by a message from a Balti take-out place in Birmingham. *Why do they insist on sending these things to people on the next continent over?* Catie thought. *Idiots . . .*

The fourth piece of "paper," though, featured a sketch of Noreen Takeuchi, a particular friend of Catie's who lived outside Seattle and whom she'd met in passing at an online software exhibition. The sketch showed Noreen rendered in "pastels," a tall, muscular girl whose mane of chestnut brown hair, tied up high in an optimistic ponytail, was always betrayed by gravity within a matter of minutes. Noreen was as hot on the art of virtual imaging as Catie was, and (to Catie's mild annoyance) was probably better at it than she was, but the two of them were too interested in sharing and comparing imaging techniques to ever develop much in the way of rivalry.

Catie picked up the page and hung it up in the air, off to one side of her chair. There it held itself flat as if pasted up against a window. "Space," she said, "is Noreen online right now?"

"Checking," said her workspace manager. It paused a moment, then said, "Online, but occupied."

"Maybe not as occupied as she looks," Catie said. "Give me voice hail."

"Hail away," said the workspace manager.

"Noreen," Catie said, "you got a moment?"

The "pastel" drawing of Noreen abruptly grew to full size and went three-dimensional, flushing into life as Noreen looked up and out of the "drawing" at Catie. Then the background changed, too, showing what looked like the depths of a forest, and Noreen in the middle of it, with the palette-routine window of the "BluePeriod" virtual rendering program hanging behind her. "Catie! I was wondering if you'd call tonight. Got a minute to look at this?"

"That long anyway," Catie said. Noreen turned to do something to her rendering, probably to save it, and Catie got up out of her chair and stepped through the drawing into Noreen's workspace.

It took her a second to get her bearings as she looked around her. "Wow," Catie said, "you've really come a long way with this. . . ."

Noreen smiled a dry smile, tired but pleased, and paused to rub her eyes. "This is really getting to be 'the forest primeval. . . .' " she said. "And I feel like I've been at it about that long."

The forest rendering in which they sat was a project for Noreen's honors art certification course at her high school in Seattle. Noreen had her eye on a degree from one of

the big art colleges after she graduated, something like the
Fine Applied Computer Arts degree that the Sorbonne and
ETZ were offering. But to even think of getting in the
doors of one of those places, you had to produce a "jour-
neyman" work of sufficient artistry to get the attention of
instructors who saw the best work of thousands of in-
sanely talented people in the course of a year, and were
in a position to pick and choose. The work genuinely had
to be art, too. There was no simply letting a "simm" program multiply the same prefabricated stylistic elements
over and over again to be dragged and dropped where you
wanted them. Instead, an artistic rendering involved the
careful choice and piece-by-piece modification of code
you wrote yourself, all of it then being fed into one of the
major rendering programs, and tweaked until the effect
was perfect.

Noreen had been working on the *Forest Primeval* for
the better part of six months now, starting with a rough
concept based in a piny mountain glade of the Black Forest in Germany. But this was a wilder version of one of
those glades: an older forest, more dangerous-feeling than
the shrinking though carefully tended Schwarzwald that
existed today. Noreen was attempting to suggest a forest
in which the original forms of this century's oversanitized
fairy tales might still be walking around in the shadows—
wolves who might actually just haul off and eat you rather
than trying to sweet-talk you first, wicked stepmothers
who wouldn't need three tries to do in a too-beautiful
stepdaughter, and castles that cast unnerving shadows
over the territory they controlled—a landscape in which
the peasants had good reason to carry torches and pitchforks. It was a wonder, this forest, for as you looked
around inside it, you could feel eyes looking at you out
of the dimness with the gold-glinting forward stare of
predators' eyes; and the shadows gathered themselves together under the deep jade-green silence of the trees, a
green that was almost black, and dared you to step into
them. Far, far up between the overhanging branches you
might every now and then catch a distant glimpse of blue
sky, but the sense of that blueness being ephemeral, and

the certainty that dark was coming on fast, grew on you as you looked. Catie shivered. The illusion was very satisfying, and it absolutely gave her the creeps.

"Wow," she said, and sat down in the pine needles to just look around her and appreciate it all. "When do you think it'll be ready?"

"When it's done," Noreen said, and sat down beside her, chuckling. Catie grinned, too, at Michelangelo's old answer to the question. "But seriously, I've got about another month at least to work on the background stuff— the subliminals and so on. And I'm still not sure I'm happy with the fractal generator for the pine needles. Too many of them are too much alike."

Catie let out an amused breath. Noreen had been rewriting the "pine needle" routine about once a week ever since she started this piece. "You're going to wind up making every one of them different," she said, "like nature."

"I don't know if that'd be a *bad* thing, necessarily," Noreen said, "but it'd mean I'd miss this year's submission deadline. . . ."

Catie shook her head, looking around her again. "Don't be an idiot," she said. "One thing's for sure, you've got the subliminal stuff handled. I can't feel anything except the shivers."

"Yeah, well, I still hate it. The great artists don't need the subliminals, they do it all with paint and electrons," Noreen said, rubbing her eyes again, "and if it weren't for the fact that I know my assessment board is going to have at least three commercial artists on it, I wouldn't bother. But if you don't put at least something subby in it, they won't think you understand the medium at all. . . ." She made a face. "Never mind them, the philistines. How's your new one coming?"

"Want to see? Come on through."

"No, it's okay, the *Forest*'s saved and frozen for the moment . . . you can display in here."

"Sure. Space, bring the *Appian Way* in here, would you?"

"Are you sure the world is ready for this?" her work-space manager said.

Noreen gave Catie an amused glance. "I'm gonna kill him," Catie said.

"Your brother?"

"Him, too, possibly. But not in this case. I let a friend tinker with my manager. Never again! Now, listen, you," Catie said in the direction of the frame of the drawing of Noreen, through which her own workspace could still be dimly seen, "just unfold that piece in here, and make it snappy, before I call NASA and see if they need a spare management system for the Styx probe. See how you like a one-way cruise to Pluto this summer."

There was no comment from her space management program, but a moment later the dark woods were all hidden away "behind" an image of a long, pillared street, paved in white travertine marble and leading down into a cityscape sprawling and glowing in mellow creams and golds. It was Rome, not the city of the year 2025 but of the year 80, lying spread out in a long summer afternoon, the faint din of half a million people dimmed down under the twin effects of distance and the mist beginning to rise from the Tiber as the day cooled lazily down. Here and there the glint of real gold highlighted the composition, gleaming from the dome of the Pantheon and the crown of the "miniature" version of the Colossus of Rhodes outside the Flavian Amphitheater, the statue that gave the neighboring building the nickname "Colosseum," and gold also shone from the tops of the masts around the great arena's circumference, from which the huge translucent "sunroof" was hung. The roof was down at the moment, the Colosseum being "dark" today, and the city lay in something like peace, the roars of the crowds silent for once. A little arrowhead of ducks flew low between two of the Seven Hills, making for a landing in the Tiber. Their passage was saluted from beneath by the screeching of the sacred geese on the Capitoline.

Noreen sat and looked it over for a few moments. "It's gorgeous," she said at last.

"I'm glad you think so," Catie muttered. "I spent all

last week hammering on the textures, but I'm still not happy. It's all too bright and shiny."

"I thought you said the Romans liked their marble shiny."

"They did, and I'd like to have this look the way the Romans really saw it. But when I turn the reflective index up that high, it looks fake. Take a look at this—"

They spent some minutes talking about the problem, while Catie pulled down an editing window from midair to change the reflectivity on some parts of the city's stone, turning it up and down, and once or twice moving the sun around to show Noreen what the problem was. Normally Catie would have been shy about debugging a project in front of someone else like this, even a friend. She preferred to exhibit perfection, or as close to it as she could get. But on the other hand, this problem had been driving Catie crazy for days. Part of the difficulty was that she preferred portraiture and detailed studies of single objects. But landscape was one of the things an imaging specialist simply had to handle well, since so much of virtual experience involved landscape design of one kind or another, and if Catie was going to become accomplished enough at this art to eventually be hired by Net Force as an imaging expert, it was just something she was going to have to master.

"I see what you mean," Noreen said after a while, sitting back on the worn stone of a little bench which had replaced the pine needles they had been sitting on. She sounded dubious. "I wish I had something to suggest. Other than—have you thought of patching in a lighting routine from a different program? Some of the routines in BluePeriod are hard to configure properly if you've got a lot of textures, the way you have in here."

Catie breathed out again. "I tried lighting out of One Ear, SuperPalette, and Effuse, but none of them made much difference."

"Hmm. Not Luau?"

"Uh, no, I don't have Luau."

"I'll lend you their lighting 'bundle'—it's transferrable

for test purposes. If you like it, register it with them, but at least you can see if it works first—"

"Catie?"

They both looked up, Catie with a look of amused annoyance. It was her brother's voice, more or less, but there was something odd about it, a lower timbre than usual. "Yeah?"

"Message for Catie Murray . . . Come in, Catie . . ."

She threw a glance at Noreen and got up, reaching into the editing window to kill her own composition's display, then snapping it up like a rollerblind to shut it. "I'd better go deal with him," Catie said, "before he follows me in here and starts messing with things. Look, I'll give you a yell tomorrow evening, huh? After I try the Luau routines out. And thanks for the help."

"Sure thing, Cates. I'll have my space send the program over."

Catie waved at Noreen and stepped back through the frame of her drawing of her friend. On the other side, back in her own space, she turned and peeled the "drawing" out of the air, then turned toward her chair . . . and did a doubletake, standing there with the drawing-gateway in her hand. Sitting in Catie's chair was a Frankenstein monster, lanky, big-foreheaded, and slightly green, but, rather unusually for Frankenstein monsters, he was dressed in white tie and tails. He looked rather uncomfortable.

"Uh. Hi, there," Catie said.

The monster got carefully to its feet, revealing a red cummerbund and, of all things, red socks under the patent-leather shoes. "My master says to tell you that it's on," said the monster, more or less in her brother's voice.

"Your *master*," Catie said, grinning. Hal's sense of humor occasionally broke out in strange forms. In this case, it was his own workspace management program speaking to her in this unusual shape. "*What's* on, exactly?"

"Your meeting with George Brickner," said the monster. Outside, Catie thought she could faintly hear the sounds of peasants with pitchforks, somewhere out on the

First Street side of the Library of Congress, and getting louder. "Saturday morning at eleven."

"Space?" Catie said.

"Awaiting your beck and call, O Mistress."

Catie's eyebrows went up. "Don't you start learning bad habits from Hal's space now," she said. "Meanwhile, make a note of the Net address for the meeting."

"Brace yourself for a shock," said her workspace, "but it's not a virtual address. Delano's, 445 P Street, Georgetown, phone—"

"Hold the phone," Catie said. *I wonder what's bringing this guy up all the way here from Florida?* she thought. *Some business to do with his team . . . ?* That had to be it. "What's Delano's? Some kind of restaurant?"

"The Yellow Spaces listing says 'diner,'" said her workspace.

"Huh," Catie said. "Maybe over by the university."

"Near Poulton Hall," said her workspace.

Catie nodded. "Okay, Boris," she said to the monster, "tell your 'master' that the message is received and understood." She waved bye-bye.

The monster bowed a finishing-school bow, during which its toupee fell off, then it vanished. Catie stood there for a moment with a wry look on her face until the sound of the peasants with pitchforks faded away. Then she bent down to pick up the toupee, flung it into the air so that it caught fire and vanished, and then set about tidying up her workspace, beckoning some of the piles of files and sketches to float in the air around her for sorting. *Now I can start finding out just why Mark Gridley was so interested in this guy,* Catie thought. *And as for whatever slight interest I might have myself . . .*

She grinned and started going through the papers in one hovering pile, idly humming "Slugs' Revenge."

3

As sometimes happened, she didn't see her parents again until the next day—her mother routinely left for work well before Catie needed to leave for school, and her father was either sleeping in after a long night's work or possibly hadn't stopped at all. Catie had paused by the studio door and listened, just before leaving for school, but hadn't heard anything, and the fact itself meant nothing. He could be either sitting and contemplating his work, or snoozing on the beat-up couch before getting up to take another run at the canvas.

It was Friday, and she only had a half day at Bradford Academy today. Catie had finished most of her finals and had only one or two more classes to deal with—mostly administrative stuff, the grading of the second-semester projects for her advanced arts class, and a final session of prep for the eleventh-grade organic chemistry final, which she was not too concerned about. For some bizarre reason, she had found organic chemistry easier to handle than the regular kind. By one o'clock she was out of class and heading down the tree-shaded street toward home.

Her brother, wearing a Banana Slugs slick-over and (bizarrely) an overall apron, was clanging around in the kitchen when Catie came in. Pots and pans were every-where, scattered all over the counters. This was something that had been happening with increasing frequency lately. Catie's mom had insisted that both her kids should be at least good enough in the kitchen to make dinner for them-selves and their dad if she was late at the library, and her brother had always been a competent cook, if not an en-thusiastic one. Lately, though, Hal had been in here a lot, much more than usual. Now he was frantically stirring what looked to Catie like a pot of nothing but near-boiling water, while feeling sideways for an egg he had already cracked onto a plate.

Catie looked curiously into the pan. "What're you mak-ing?"

"Eggs Benedict. Don't distract me, this is for school."

Catie blinked at that. He had finished his home arts course last year. "Which class?"

"Chemistry." He stirred faster and dumped the egg off the plate into the pan. "Don't bug me now, Catie, this is important!"

"Eggs Benedict? For *chemistry*?" But her brother didn't say anything, just stopped stirring and watched the egg slip down to the bottom of the vortex he had created and, whirling there, begin to poach.

Catie shook her head, wondering what on earth they'd done to the tenth-grade chemistry syllabus since she'd taken it, and turned away to dump her bookbag on the table. As she turned she saw that her father was leaning his tall rangy self against one side of the kitchen doorway, scrubbing thoughtfully at his hands with a turp-soaked rag while he watched Hal's performance. He was, as usual, dressed in work clothes—jeans that had already been old and tired early in the century and were now washed and faded nearly to white, and on top an ancient and faded T-shirt featuring a stripe-beaked toucan standing on sten-ciled letters that read GUINNESS. Also as usual, like his work, her father and his clothes were all colors of the rainbow, an abstract pseudo-Impressionist study in smears and smudges. Warren Murray had won much critical ac-claim over his career for his "luminous and inventive use of color." At the moment, though, the inventiveness seemed mostly to consist of getting it into his dark thinning hair in ways only nervously contemplated by other, lesser artists. Catie looked at her dad and shook her head, knowing what her mother was going to say about the laundry in a day or two, not to mention the carmine streak radiating jaggedly back from his parted hair on the right side.

"Daddy," she said, "why don't you at least change over to acrylics?"

He looked up at Catie and smiled slightly, a tired look on that long face of his, but a satisfied one. "They just don't get the same color saturation as oils, honey, you know that. . . ."

"Did you even sleep last night?"

"Eventually, yeah." But she could see that he hadn't actually stopped work, since he was only now cleaning up. "I crashed out on the studio couch. I knew I was almost done, and there wasn't any point in cleaning up. Finished now, though."

Catie went into the fridge for the ever-present pitcher of iced tea, and also brought out a bottle of Duvel for her dad. When he finished a piece of work, he routinely allowed himself a beer to celebrate. "You really should use electrons instead of paint," she said, handing him the little wire-stoppered bottle and turning to get the specially shaped Duvel glass and a tumbler for her iced tea out of the cupboard over the sink. "It wouldn't get all over the couch."

"It's all electrons when you come down to it," her father said. "It's just that some of them are wetter than others." He started to push back the one lock of forehead hair that always got in his way, and then paused, looking at the blue and green paint that was still all over the back of that hand. He started scrubbing at it with the rag, then pushed the rag into his pocket and turned his attention to getting the Duvel bottle open.

"What were you doing?"

Hal, peering into the pot he had been stirring, now began to speak in some language that certainly wasn't English, and from the sound of it didn't involve concepts that Catie was eager to have translated. Apparently something had gone wrong in the pan. Her father raised his eyebrows and said, "Come on down and see. We can get out of Escoffier's way."

Catie followed him down the hall past the bedrooms and into the studio. Its door was open, and the smell of oil paint and linseed oil was still strong, though she could hear the air purifier working all-out to get rid of it. This time of day the north light that came in through the back windows and the skylight was at its best, the sun having swung around the other side of the house. In the middle of the room, well away from the Net access box and the implant chair, under the spots and within range of the digital rendering camera, a canvas stood on an easel blotched with every conceivable color of paint.

It was a piece of background work, one on which text would be superimposed during a virtcast, a swirl and rush of blues and greens . . . but there was more to it than that. "Dry yet?" Catie said.

"You kidding? We can put a colony on the moon, but we can't develop a drying agent for oils that works faster than twenty-four hours. . . ."

"This is the one for CNNSI?"

"Yeah, for the FINA swimming championships next year." They stood back together and regarded the canvas. On first glance, an unsuspecting viewer might have called the work an abstract. But then, as your glance sank into the greens and blues and viridians of it, you began to perceive the flashes of hotter, brighter color half-submerged in the glassy hues, streaks and submerged ripples of red and gold, and you got a sense of splashing strength, shapes cutting the water or plunging into it, all going somewhere at speed. The effect was subtle, and yet the longer you looked at it, the more you saw swimmers and divers, moving—even in so static a medium.

"They'll want me to animate it, of course," her father said, and raised his eyebrows in an expression that said, clearly enough, *The idiots!* "Probably they'll want it to ripple like water. If they had the brains God gave bluepoint oysters, they'd notice that if you just sit still and look at it for more than five seconds, your brain'll begin producing that effect itself." He gave Catie a wry sidelong look. "But getting even the art director to sit still that long, these days, is a challenge. Not to mention the virtual audience, who are going to have to view the work nearly completely covered with flashing crawling text, in a window that they may keep sized down to the size of a postage stamp in the virtual 'field of view,' half the time . . . so the art director is going to insist that there be something about it that moves, to remind the viewers that it's there." Her dad turned to look at the canvas again. "If I'm unlucky, the thing is going to wind up looking like an ad for toilet bowl cleaner by the time they're through. If I'm lucky . . ." He sighed, and shrugged.

Catie stepped closer to look at the way her father had layered the paint over the flash of color that was meant to represent a swimmer. The palette knife had been involved, which was probably the scraping Hal had heard last night. "You'll get some 'print' sales, though. . . ."

"Oh, yeah," her dad said, taking a long drink of the Duvel, and smiling slightly. "The collectors will notice it when it airs. And anyway, there are always people who suddenly notice a nice graphic for the first time and want a copy for their workspace. We'll do okay from that."

Catie looked at the work for a moment. There was more speed inherent in it than just that of swimmers and divers. "You were in a hurry on this one. . . ." she said.

Her father started to push his hair back again, and stopped himself, laughed, and had another drink of beer. "Yes. It's not due yet, but I want to get the stuff in before deadline . . . so I can get well ahead on the next commission, and have plenty of time to sort everything out and clean up in here before the builders arrive." His expression showed that he was already dreading the incursion.

Catie shook her head. "You should do what Mom suggested, and reschedule the builders for later. Then we could all go away somewhere for a week, while the place is all torn up. Up to the Jersey Shore, maybe . . . or over to Assateague . . ."

Her father looked thoughtful. Then he shook his head. "Nope. The sooner it's done, the sooner I can get back to work."

Catie smiled slightly. It was easy to forget sometimes how much her father loved what he did, when most of her classmates could talk about nothing but how their folks disliked their jobs and couldn't wait to get away on vacation. If she was lucky, some day she would be in the same position, when she got a job at Net Force. She refused to think of it in terms of *if*.

And that reminded her. "Oh," Catie said, "I was going to tell you last night, but you were busy. Hal's friend the spatball player from South Florida Spat is going to be in town tomorrow . . . we're going into Georgetown to see him at lunch."

"Hey, that's great for you. You need a ride?"

She shook her head. "We'll go public . . . between the Metro and the tram, it's not a problem."

"This is their big star, huh?"

"So I hear. A lot of people are interested in South Florida all of a sudden . . . I assume that's why he's coming up here in the first place."

He nodded, having another drink of his beer and looking at the painting. ". . . Why do you think they're so popular just now?"

Catie looked at her father quizzically. "You getting interested in sports all of a sudden?" she said. It was an unusual concept, for though he might render sports themes in the course of his work, he wasn't particularly a fan of any of them. In fact, her dad routinely claimed that his introduction to commercial art was when he learned to forge his parents' signatures on "notes from home" asking that he be excused from gym; and later, until he was caught, he had run a small but lucrative business forging other kids' parents' signatures at five bucks a shot.

"Me? Sports? Not a chance," Catie's father said. "But the psychology of this particular situation . . . maybe."

Catie thought about that. "I don't know for sure," she said. "It could just be the underdog thing, I guess. People enjoy seeing an unlikely winner taking on the 'big guys.' "

Her father nodded, pulled out the turpentine rag again, and sat down on the poor beat-up, paint-spattered couch, where he started scrubbing once more at the back of his left hand, where it was still blue and green. "Maybe. I guess I'm not clear on how they managed it in the first place, though."

"If I understand it right," Catie said, leaning against the tube- and bottle-cluttered desk near the studio door, "somebody in the first organizing body of the sport actually had the brains to set themselves up as a licensing body as well, to make sure they kept control over it. I don't understand most of the legal stuff, but I think Hal told me they *had* to do that in order to get permission to keep using cubic on the International Space Station for those first few tournaments. He said the first organizers wanted to make sure the sport didn't lose the amateur feel, even when it started to get professionalized—they were smart enough to see that coming over the horizon, eventually—and when the league structure started to be set up, they wrote it specifically into the structure document that Spat International would not allow strictly professional leagues. They could call themselves something else if they went professional, but they couldn't call it 'spatball.' "

Her father nodded slowly. "You're telling me they decided to license the brand, as much as the game itself." He chucked the rag into the little self-sealing ceramic garbage can nearby where his flammable disposables went, and picked up his beer glass again. "Possibly a very smart move."

"Seems that way," Catie said. "Hal says the big teams have tried a couple different ways to break the license or weasel around it, and every time they try, they get blown out of the water in one jurisdiction or another. Apparently the player who drew up the structure document as part of the original license was also a lawyer with a specialty in international trademark and patent law, and he really knew what he was doing."

"Huh," her father said, having another drink of Duvel.

"But this is still kind of unusual, I take it."

"Oh, yeah," Catie said. "The structure of the yearly spat schedule usually seems to shake out all but the very best teams early on, and mostly the ones who're left are the professional teams. Partly it's because the professionals have lots of money to recruit the most talented players from the semipro and amateur teams. Seems like the semis and amateurs have been complaining about that for a long time. In the normal course of the competitions, most of the amateur teams usually fall by the wayside by the mid-season break. But not this one. . . ."

Her father finished his beer, got up, and picked up the rag can, glancing one last time at the painting. "Well," he said, "it's going to be interesting to see how the rest of the season unfolds for South Florida. I would imagine the pressure on them is increasing to levels they wouldn't normally experience as a purely amateur team."

Catie nodded as they walked back toward the kitchen. "That's sort of why I want to meet their team captain," she said.

Her father raised his eyebrows at her as they went into the kitchen and he kept going, toward the door that led to the garage, the side of the house, and the sealed disposal for the flammable garbage. "So you're telling me that it really *doesn't* have anything to do with the fact that *People* described this guy as having 'the best physical aspects of a young god'?"

He was out the door before Catie could think of an appropriate response to that. Her brother was still stirring the same pot he had been stirring before, looking both intent and angry, and he was reaching for another egg-on-a-dish.

"*Chemistry?*" Catie said, looking at him in complete bemusement.

"Blast yourself out of here," Hal said, not looking up, "before I call whichever public agency is in charge of having a close relative's body donated to science."

Smiling slightly, Catie went on down the hall to her room to change out of her school clothes.

• • •

About a hundred and fifty miles away, in the top-floor lobby bar of the Marriott Hilton Parkway in Philadelphia, two men sat across a low bar table and looked down the length of Ben Franklin Parkway, toward the faux-Greek, painted portico of the art museum. Two long lines of trees stretched up the parkway toward Museum Circle, but not a breath of wind stirred them. Every leaf hung still and flat-looking in the heat and the odd light. In the west, thunderclouds were piling up in curdling heaps of white and livid blue, threatening one of those four o'clock thunderstorms to which Philly is prone in most summers. But it was some time from happening yet, and everything outside the big floor-to-ceiling windows of the bar lay in a breathless, panting stillness of heat and humidity, waiting for the storm to break.

The two men who sat there in the bar and looked down the parkway, rather than at one another, were both wearing dark clothes in cuts that were designed not to stand out in any particular way. They had taken off their sunglasses because wearing sunglasses inside was a good way to make you stand out, and they were both drinking nondescript drinks that might or might not have had alcohol in them, to the casual observer.

It was the first time the two men had met nonvirtually, and they had made the discovery about each other that so many people make in such circumstances—that the seeming each of them routinely wore was an almost exact opposite of his real appearance, and therefore could have been used to predict one another's genuine appearance, if either one had been bothered to try. Darjàn turned out to be a short fair man, a little on the bulky side, with hair surprisingly long for the styles that year; and Heming turned out to be tall and slim to the point of boniness, swarthy, and with very close-cropped dark hair. The revelation did not move either of them to like the other one any more . . . and it would hardly have been possible for them to like one another less, especially since circumstances had forced them to meet nonvirtually, and thereby lose whatever cover their seemings had until now provided them.

"Anyway, we made contact with one of his people," Heming was saying. "He was coming up here on business anyway. We'll see him tomorrow afternoon."

"Watch where he goes," said Darjan.

Heming looked bemused at that. "Of course we would. But . . . you don't think he's intending to make contact with some other organization . . . do you?"

"If he's smart he won't," said Darjan. "If he's smart he'll play ball strictly with us, on the one side . . . and leave everybody else strictly alone, on the other. But I'm sure he knows better than to go to anyone else, anyway. It's not as if the offer he's been made is a bad one."

"Unless . . ." Heming looked suddenly concerned. "Unless he's decided to jump into the arms of some law-enforcement organization or another. . . ."

They both sat quite still for a moment. Then Darjan shook his head.

"He wouldn't be so stupid. It would be suicidal. Anyway, he could tell them anything he liked, but there'd be no evidence to back the claim. We've been most careful to cover ourselves completely in all our dealings with him." He lifted the frosty glass sitting on the table and sipped at it, put it down again. "No," Darjan said at last. "I don't see it as being a problem. Nonetheless . . . keep an eye on his whereabouts for the next few days, until we have a result that favors what our principals want, and things begin to settle down."

They looked down the parkway. The leaves of the trees were starting to stir a little now. "How are the principals doing?" Heming said.

Darjan paused a good while before replying. "They're twitching. What do you expect? Even in years when things go according to plan, they twitch. There are always factors they can't control in the other sports they run. Weather, civil unrest, player injuries . . . But this is worse, in a way, because it could have been controlled further down the line, if anyone had thought it was necessary. No one did. Now . . ." Darjan trailed off. "Now it's too late, and matters can't just be allowed to take their course. Now people have to start getting involved to stop it. And the upper-ups hate having to do anything that looks like involvement. It's too easy to leave a trace, a trail. . . ."

The sky was darkening, going not so much gray as a weird kind of bruise-green, and slowly the wind continued to rise. "Well," Heming said, "after tomorrow, when we lay down the law . . . and also the reward for doing what he's told . . . you should be able to tell them to stop worrying. Between that, and what Chicago should do to them in a few days, a lot of people should be pretty relieved."

"So the arrangements are in place for the tournament 'cubic,' then. . . ."

Darjan stretched. "They're just there for experiment's sake at the moment. The intervention is expected to be minimal at best. We may not even need them. Shouldn't, if Chicago delivers. If we do need to use them . . ." He shrugged. "We'll use them judiciously enough that no one will suspect anything. It's a test, as I said. For possible use elsewhere."

They were both silent for the moment as the bar waiter came around by their table, making his rounds through the lounge space. "Anything, gentlemen?"

They shook their heads. The waiter went off to one of the few other tables that was presently occupied. It was one of the reasons the two of them were here—this place tended to be quiet in the afternoons. When he was well out of range, Darjan said, "The game is two o'clock Sunday. Without overtime and with the usual breaks between the halves, it'll be over around four-thirty. I'll be expecting to hear from you at five. And so will *they*."

Heming nodded. He reached down and picked up his glass again, jingling the ice cubes in it a little. "Chicago," he said.

Darjan nodded once and held up his glass as well, but didn't clink it with Heming's. Heming gave him a look, waiting. Finally he drank.

A wild electric flicker came from down the parkway in the direction of the art museum, followed by a long rumble of thunder that rolled up the parkway on a sudden, gusty bluster of wind; and behind it, pelting down diagonally, came the rain.

Heming shivered, and finished his drink.

• • •

The next morning Catie got up much earlier than she strictly had to on a Saturday. Partly it was to get some chores done, for over the last few days, she had somewhat slighted her attention to the chores roster that her mother had left written on the slick white LivePad faired into the refrigerator door. Specifically, the word *lawn*, which had been there by itself on the LivePad on Tuesday, had additionally been circled sometime on Wednesday, and on Thursday had had many flashing arrows in various colors drawn pointing to it. Then, some time last night, it had developed an alarming number of exclamation points which alternately flashed red and blue like some kind of warning from the local emergency services. Her mom might nag, Catie thought as she got the lawn mower out of the garage around nine, but at least she did it in a way that made you laugh rather than want to leave home.

The mower was a John Deere "Hunter," powered by photovoltaic panels on the top, and normally mowing the lawn was just a matter of taking it out of the garage, putting the meter-square box-on-wheels out on the grass, and turning it loose. The border sensors and the onboard motor normally did the rest—though there was one spot near the corner of the front lawn where you had to watch the thing, especially if the lawn was fairly overgrown, as it was today. For some reason, under such conditions, the mower tended to roll out onto the sidewalk or the driveway, get itself confused, and then either run out into the street looking for more lawn, or make its way over to the next-door neighbor's lawn and start mowing *that*. However, at eight in the morning, with the sun still low behind the trees, there wasn't enough light yet to power the photovoltaics, so Catie had to fit the battery pack module to the mower body before she set it out on the lawn and hit the Go button on the remote.

The mower trundled off, its cutter buzzing, and Catie sat down on the front steps to keep an eye on it, at least until it was away from the spot where it liked to stage the Great Escape. She rubbed her eyes. Even after her shower, they felt a little grainy. She had spent a good while last night looking over various articles and vids about South Florida Spat in the sports press, and some excerpts from virtcasts which she had earlier instructed her workspace to find and save for her. Interest in the team was certainly building fast. One story suggested that the team, which hadn't been able to secure any corporate sponsorship at all a year or two ago, was now being wooed by some of the biggest sportswear companies, and offered very lucrative support packages if only South Florida would include their logos on its virtual spat uniform . . . excluding all the other companies, of course. What seemed to be surprising the sports commentators, though, as much as the big companies themselves, was that South Florida had so far turned down all these offers. No one seemed to know what to make of this.

The mower came up to the low box hedge on the left side of the front lawn, turned left and left again, and began to mow a stripe parallel to the one it had just done, closest to the sidewalk. Catie watched it carefully. *It's almost as if they can't understand any team that doesn't behave exactly the way all the professional ones do*, she thought. *Like they find it impossible to believe that an amateur team wouldn't automatically* want *to be professional, the first chance it got.*

The mower came to the end of the strip it was mowing, and, sure enough, rolled out onto the sidewalk and started heading for the Kowalskis' lawn next door. "Oh, no, you don't!" Catie muttered, pointing the remote at it and hitting the right-arrow key for "turn."

The mower kept going.

"Technology," Catie said under her breath, disgusted, and went after the mower, hitting the Stop button on the remote as she did so. The mower ignored this, too, and she just managed to catch up with it and hit the master power button on the upper surface before it rolled up onto the Kowalskis' grass. The mower's motor buzzed down to silence, and Catie picked it up and took it back to her own lawn, trying to hold it a little away so she wouldn't get grass clippings all over herself. "What's the matter with you, you hunk of junk?" she said. "Is your code buggy somewhere, I wonder . . . ?"

Catie put the mower back on the lawn, next to the stripe that it had completed and at the end of which it had escaped, then hit the power switch again and turned it loose once more. Off it went, and this time she stood and watched it while it trundled down the length of the lawn, across the flagstones that led to the front door, and down to the hedge, where it turned. The mower then came back, crossed the flagstones again, came to the driveway, and this time sensed it correctly—turned, and headed for the hedge again.

Catie sat back down on the steps and kept watching the mower. Her viewing last night of South Florida's recent history and the professional reaction to it had left her with a feeling of pressure. The whole array of the "paid" part of the sport drawn up and looming over this single, strange, maverick, little splinter group, trying to force it into the shape that all the other parts of it had assumed— had perhaps been forced to assume?—over the past decade or so. She wondered how South Florida was going to react to this. For her own part, it seemed to Catie that there had to be a level on which there was still room for human beings to just do sports for the love of the sport itself. That was a concept that the commentators seemed to be having trouble with, though they claimed otherwise, and the professionals seemed to be trying to pretend that the money was somehow an accident that had happened to them—if a very nice one—and that anyone who tried to avoid that accident when it finally threatened to befall *them* was either crazy, or trying to make the professionals look bad, or trying to cheat their own team out of the recognition (Catie read this as code for "financial success") that was somehow naturally their right by becoming good enough at what they did to compete with the pros. The whole business made Catie twitch, and she was getting more and more curious to see what George Brickner's take on it was going to be.

A few more turns up and down the lawn finally saw the mower finished with its work. Catie stopped the mower with the remote, which worked this time, and got up to head into the garage again, pausing to check the top of the battery pack. Its LED gauge was still well up in the green. She went into the garage, got the grass basket, hooked it to the back of the mower, and sent it on its way again, this time set for "reverse pattern" and "vacuum."

Catie had to empty the grass basket three times. *My fault,* she thought, lugging the basket to the "compost" garbage can the second time. *I should have done this Tuesday, and not let the lawn get to the point where it looked like the Amazonian rain forest.* Then she spent another fifteen minutes or so sweeping up the cuttings that had fallen in the driveway, and generally cleaning up after herself. As she was finishing, she turned and saw her brother standing in the open front door, barefoot, wearing black sweatpants and a Glo-Shirt apparently just out of the wash, for it had reverted to the default black background and the words YOUR MESSAGE HERE, which now marched their way around Hal's upper body in white block letters. Hal was yawning. "I love work," he said as Catie came up the steps. "I could watch you do it all day."

Catie didn't say anything, since this sentiment too clearly matched her own assessment of her brother, and she didn't want to pick a fight with him right now as much as she wanted her breakfast. "This diner or whatever it is we're going to," she said, "how's the food?"

Hal followed her into the kitchen. "If it's the same as it was when I went there last, a few months ago, it's just the usual deli stuff. They had pretty good 'smoked meat' sandwiches—they get the meat from some chain in Montreal."

"Okay." Catie went to the freezer and pulled out a packaged pair of MicroCroissants, stuck them in the microwave, started zapping them, and then got herself down a mug and a teabag. It was just something light to hold her until closer to lunchtime. "Better get yourself into the shower, then. It's pushing ten already, and if we're going to get down there in time—"

"Nag, nag, nag," Hal said. "You're as bad as Mom." He headed out of the kitchen, down toward the bathroom.

Catie smiled slightly, unclipped the stylus from beside the LivePad on the fridge, and neatly crossed out the word *lawn* on the chores list. The LivePad played a small triumphant trumpet voluntary and said in her mom's voice, "Thank you, sweetie!" The word !!!*dishwasher*!!! underneath it, still untouched, then immediately developed many small red, yellow, and blue arrows pointing at it, and the word *Hal!!!* appeared nearby.

Catie just smiled and went off to make her tea.

An hour later they were at Delano's in Georgetown, a very standard Formica-and-stainless-steel–type diner, and as they came in the front door, there he was, standing by the PLEASE WAIT TO BE SEATED sign just inside the door—George Brickner. Catie was surprised to find that the man was not smaller than he seemed in virtuality, which was usually the case, but that he was taller. Five eleven easily, maybe a hundred and eighty pounds, broad-shouldered and narrow-waisted, but not so much so that he looked overmuscled, he stood there in neodenims and one of the big floppy semitrans shirts that were popular for hot-weather wear at the moment, looking pleasant, accessible, and absolutely ordinary. Hal and Catie introduced themselves, and George shook their hands and said, "Look, I'm starving, I missed my breakfast, and I couldn't eat what they were serving on the plane. It looked like a by-product of a biowar attack. Would it seem incredibly rude to you if we just sat right down and ordered something?"

"No problem at all," Hal said. "But where's Mike?"

"Late, probably," George said. "He's been late for everything ever since I've known him. He'll probably be late for his own funeral, if I know Mike. Let's just sit down. It's crazy to stand here hoping he'll turn up in the next few minutes. We'll be chewing our own elbows off by the time he gets here, if we wait for him."

The waitress came along and brought them to a booth by a window, nearly walking into things a couple of times as she tried to both go forward and at the same time talk to George while he followed her. Catie saw the heads of people seated on either side turn as the three of them passed, their eyes resting first on Brickner and then on her and Hal with an expression that seemed to read, "The first guy, we recognize. Are these two somebody important, too?" It was an odd sensation, and after the first twinge of amusement and excitement, she wasn't sure she liked it.

The three of them sat down with their menus and exchanged a few words while they looked them over. Hal did most of the talking at this point, and Catie was glad to let him do so. Until she got a feeling for what Brickner was interested in talking about and could participate in the conversation intelligently, she didn't want to sound like she was just along to see what he looked like . . . and that would be the immediate assumption, certainly of her brother, if not of George himself. For the moment, while they looked at the menus, Hal and George seemed content to tell each other stories about Mike being late for things; and after a few minutes of this, the waitress came around to take their orders. Catie asked for one of the smoked-meat sandwiches and a Coke. Hal ordered iced tea and eggs Benedict, and once again Catie wondered what on earth the dish had to do with his chemistry class.

"And for you, Mr. Brickner?" said the waitress, and positively fluttered her eyelashes at him.

Catie had a hard time keeping herself from simply laughing out loud.

"A BLT, please," George said, "and an iced tea."

"Right," the waitress said. "Thanks. Oh, and we're all big fans of yours here. . . ."

"Thanks, miss, uh"—he peered at her nametag—"thanks, Wendy. It's always good to know people are rooting for the team."

The waitress smiled and hurried off. "Looks like the service's gonna be good," Hal said, sounding dry, as she went away.

George waggled his eyebrows in a resigned way. "It's good everywhere," he said. "I just wish I knew when it was really because of the team, instead of that dratted feature in *People*."

This had been somewhat on Catie's mind as well, for

now, sitting across from the man, she was coming to the conclusion that the *People* virtzine feature might actually have had a point about George's looks. He really was a fabulous-looking guy, close up. Yet it wasn't something that sprang out at you when you saw him play. *What was it about putting this man into a uniform,* Catie thought, *that so completely changed him?* In street clothes he could pass for a model. But it was strange how that quality of sheer male beauty somehow didn't come through while watching him playing spat. It was as if the energy spent on being handsome—if one could actually be considered to "spend" personal energy on such a thing—was completely channeled into the game while George was playing, leaving him merely good-looking in a cool and uninvolved kind of way. Once he was out of the cubic, that energy seemed to be released for other purposes. Catie could now understand the annoyance of some of George's fans that he was eligible but seemingly uninterested in dating right now. For her own part, she simply amused herself with enjoying George's handsomeness as if he were some kind of walking art installation, and tried as hard as she could to remind herself that she didn't intend to get seriously involved with men at all until after she graduated from college. Unfortunately it was at times like this that the resolve seemed dumbest.

Catie blinked and came back to the moment as their drinks arrived. *Whoa,* she thought, *not like you to phase out just because of a pretty face, kid. Sharpen up!*

"Wasn't there going to be someone else here with you?" Hal was saying.

"Oh, yeah, my team cocaptain, Rick Menendez. But he's off seeing his sister in Rockville. She had a baby last week, her first, and it's his first chance to see his nephew in the flesh, instead of in a virtmail. Hilarious . . . the grimmest guy you ever saw, most of the time. He's gone all gooey." George grinned, and the flash of it made Catie smile, too, just at the sight of it. "But the whole team is up here at the moment . . . those who're going to be playing tomorrow, anyway. We're short a couple of bodies. Two nights ago we lost one of our second-string players to an invigilation call-up, would you believe? And another one has a dual qualification as an umpire, and has to go umpire a Western Division game at the same time we'll be playing Chicago and Moscow Spartak tomorrow—there's a shortage of officials right now." He shrugged. "Bad luck, I guess, but we'll cope."

"I don't think you must be very happy about having to travel the day before a game," Catie said. "Especially one this important for the team."

"Yes, well," George said, making a slightly sour face, "this is also the time at which we're running 'hottest' in terms of publicity . . . and therefore this is the time to go strike the sponsorship deal we've been waiting for. We have to go up to AirDyne's corporate headquarters in Bethesda this afternoon and do a big press conference performance. . . . It'll be all over the evening news. This kind of thing makes the ISF happy, even if it isn't our favorite thing. It'll push the 'gate' up for the game tomorrow. But we're going to be up late practicing tonight. . . ."

"I thought you didn't want a sponsorship deal," Hal said. "You've been turning them all down."

"Well," George said, "we do actually start to need sponsorship, to play at this level. The team is pretty much agreed on this. But we've also agreed that we don't want any sponsorship agreement to be *exclusive* . . . at least, not by the sponsor's choice. At our level, it probably will be, because we don't need *that* much sponsorship. One big company is plenty. And besides, there are teams that really go overboard in that regard. They get the idea that if a little money is a good idea, then more is better . . . and as a result, some of their team jerseys are so cluttered with logos you can hardly make out a color underneath them." George took a pull on his iced tea. "But more to the point, none of us on the team likes the implication—the companies don't come right out and say it, of course, though it's there—that the sponsor starts to own you, somehow, that it's okay for them to start dictating to you about tactics and play, once you've signed on the dotted line."

George sighed then. "So finally we found a sponsor that

wouldn't insist on exclusivity, and which agreed to stay out of our way on managerial issues, which was terrific. It's not like the team can't use the money. Our yearly contribution to the ISF isn't peanuts, by any means. But the Federation has to keep the Net servers where we play our games up and running somehow, and that takes hardware hosting and software maintenance and a hundred other things that all cost money. The only alternative, play in reality, is beyond any of us at the moment, even the biggest and best funded of the professional teams. Real cubic in space is just too limited and too expensive right now. It's kind of sad. It would be nice if there was at least *someplace* where the sport could be played as it was originally conceived, in genuine microgravity. But without that option, virtual's as close as we can get . . . and it's going to be that way for a long while, until the cost of nonindustrial volume in space comes down. Maybe when the L5-1 gets built, there'll be spat cubic in there. It would seem to make sense, since even in a rotating L5 there's going to be plenty of micrograv volume, especially for the big manufacturers. But that option's twenty years away, easily, and right now we have right-now problems to solve. . . ."

"Like Chicago," Hal muttered.

"Chicago," said George, "we'll solve the old-fashioned way. We'll beat them. They have tactical weaknesses that we can exploit, and besides, O'Mahony got herself her third yellow card in that last game. Careless of her. Bad coaching, as much as anything else. Her coach lets her lose her temper and get away with it. One more foul like that, and we won't have her to worry about anymore. . . ."

Their food arrived. Catie found herself looking with faint dismay at one of the biggest sandwiches she had ever seen in her life. The thing was nearly nine inches tall, and she had never seen such a forlorn and pitiful statement as the single toothpick pushed into the top of it, pretending to hold it all together. There was easily what looked like half a cow's worth of smoked meat in there. She sighed, picked up half of it, pushed out some of the meat, reassembled it, then squashed it into some thickness she hoped she could at least get a bite out of and went to work.

George's sandwich was cast in much the same mold, and for a few minutes quiet mostly prevailed as he and Catie jointly tried to get their lunches under control, while Hal tucked into his eggs Benedict. "You're mostly a new fan, I take it," George said to Catie after a while, taking a break from his sandwich.

Catie nodded. "Yeah. Until now I've been playing soccer, mostly," she said.

"Real or virtual?"

"Real. Local-league level."

George flashed that brilliant smile at her again. "A rugged individualist, in this day and age, to play out on the grass under the sun, and get yourself burned and banged up."

Catie shook her head. "It's just reaction to the rest of my life. The soccer's a good way to stay in touch with physical reality. I do so much virtual stuff: schoolwork of course, and a lot of imaging, and Net Force Explorers . . . and some F.I.C.E.-sponsored chess, in the winter, when you'd have to be crazy to play anything outdoors."

That got another smile out of George, an impressed one. "Really? Plane or 3-D?"

"Plane. I prefer the classic approach."

"What level?"

"Three. Nothing to brag about."

"I made three once," George said, "when I was in my teens. But I didn't have what it took for tournament play. Physical stuff turned out to be more my forte. I did some track and field . . . then I found spat. Or it found me—"

"You couldn't have waited, could you?" said a voice from down the aisle of the restaurant. They all looked up. A stocky fair-haired guy about Hal's height but about twice his width, and maybe twenty years old, was standing by their table and looking over their meals with a critical eye.

"Late as always," George said, glancing at him and picking up his sandwich again. "Nothing for *you*. We ate yours."

"Oh, *yeah*, Bird," said Mike, completely unconcerned, sitting down next to George as George pushed over to make room for him. "Hey, Hal, how's it going? How'd that test go?"

"Aced it."

"Good for you . . . we'll get you into Brown yet. This your sister?"

"Yup. Catie, this is Mike Manning."

"Hi, Catie, nice to meet you. Is there a menu?" Mike started looking around him, and a second later Wendy the waitress had materialized at the table, smiling, and was handing him one. Mike asked for a lemonade fizz; she went off to get it like she'd been waiting for the request her whole life.

While Mike was looking over the menu, Catie glanced over at George. "There's a question I'd like to ask you. . . ."

Mike hooted with laughter and elbowed George.

George raised his eyebrows. "No," he said, with the slightest smile, "I'm not married, I'm not dating, I'm not gay, and I have no plans."

Catie grinned, but she couldn't stop herself from blushing, regardless. "Not that one," she said. "Why, exactly, do they call you 'The Parrot'?"

"Oh," George said, and threw Mike a look. "See that? There's your one in a hundred. You owe me a nickel."

Mike flipped over the menu to look at the other side. "I'll have it transferred to your account," he said, grinning.

George turned back to Catie with a chuckle. "You can guess how often I hear a different question. Never mind. The name's a compliment."

"Oh?" Catie said. She was now completely bemused.

"It's an in-joke," George said. "You know how it was when they finally got the International Space Station built, or the first phase of it anyway, before the private finance came in to double the thing's cubic? Very official, very military and shipshape. Well, they'd brought some animals up for testing on and off, but there was a 'no pets' policy for a long time. Understandable, I guess. At that point they didn't have the recycling system in, or that much space for spare food and water; and besides, with animals there were some elimination problems in microgravity. . . ." He smiled a little. "Then the Selective Spin module was added on for the crystal-growth and metallurgical research and the manufacturing pilot project; and people started playing spat in the main sphere before it was populated. While that was happening, one of the project biologists set up this convoluted research project that had to do with magnetic field orientation in birds, and it called for birds to be brought up to the station and reared in microgravity to see how it affected their flight characteristics and directional sense and so on." George gave Catie an amused look. "And he made a big case that the birds brought up for this should be highly intelligent, and used to confinement. So what do you think the experiment wound up using?"

"Uh . . . Parakeets."

"Close. Parrots. But more to the point, gray parrots . . . and most specifically, a pair of breeding parrots that belonged to the biologist. George and Gracie, they were called. African greys, very intelligent, very long-lived, everyone agreed with that . . . but they were also his pets."

Catie snickered. At that point Wendy arrived again to take Mike's order, for a minute steak and fries, and paused to bat her eyelashes at George before going off again. Mike watched her go, impressed. "I've never seen that technique outside of old cartoons," he said. "A new one for the collection."

"Yeah," George said. "Well . . . anyway . . . the parrots. There was some noise about them, but the project had been approved by some NASA suits who didn't know they were being scammed, and the project managers for the station had the choice of either letting the project go through, or giving the money back. And no one on the station wanted to do that. It was hard enough to get sponsorship for any kind of research at all at that point, unless it was specifically commercial. And giving research money back unused is *always* a bad move. It makes the people who gave it to you think maybe they should routinely give you less. So . . . anyway . . . the parrots came up on the shuttle and lived there for about five years, and they did fine. They bred, too, which was a good thing, otherwise the project biologist would have been in a lot of trouble. But what was really terrific was how the young parrots took to life in space. All the little Georges and Gracies evolved a whole new way of flying. Spatball players still study the films that Harry—that was the biologist—made of his birds and their offspring. So do astronauts. The chicks found out things about maneuvering in microgravity within their first few weeks of life that even trained astronauts took a lot longer to work out for themselves. And obviously the parents learned, too . . . but their learning curve was a lot like the human astronauts'; they made the same kind of mistakes at the same kind of speed."

George leaned back and took a drag of his iced tea. "Now the moral of the story," he said, "is that among the other things Harry the biologist used to do, was play spatball. In fact, he was a member of one of the very first 'real space' teams that formed to play in the Selective Spin cubic before it was populated and the game had to go virtual. And his birds played with them. George and Gracie in particular liked to get into the games and follow their boss around . . . George even more than Gracie. So that, these days, if you're any good as a spatball player, and you're named George, you are pretty much condemned to be referred to as 'The Parrot.'" He raised his eyebrows, producing a resigned expression. "It's hardly anything new. But since we hit the news, suddenly it's a big deal."

Catie shook her head. She was unable to stop thinking about some of the side effects of having pet birds, at least one of which had repeatedly occurred to her when as a youngster she'd gotten stuck with cage-cleaning for a pair of parakeets that her brother had lost interest in. "I can see where it would happen. But, George, what about . . ."

". . . the stuff parrots usually leave on the bottom of their cages, getting all over a space station?" George laughed. "It didn't. They just housebroke the parrots."

"You're kidding."

"No, seriously. It's apparently not that hard to do. It's partly a matter of controlling when they eat and what they eat, and partly reinforcing good behavior. See, I know a lot about this because of the nickname, because every-body—*everybody!*—asks that question as soon as they can."

Catie laughed. "Okay," she said. "So now I've done at least *one* thing that was expected of me."

"Thank heaven. Now we can get on with life."

"Which means the next game," Hal said.

George picked up the second half of his sandwich. "There is more to life," said George mildly, "than the next game. Though you wouldn't think that CNNSI believed it. Or any of the other news services that've been camped out around my apartment lately, or the Miami area in general . . . especially the sports news services. They seem to think it's bizarre beyond belief that I do my own shopping. Like, now that we're in the championships, suddenly a personal shopper should descend from the heavens and start taking care of me." He laughed, but it had a slightly despairing sound to it. "I caught the guy from AB/CBS going through my garbage the other day. For *what*? Clues about my training diet? To see what junk mail I throw out? He wouldn't tell me! I told him he wasn't allowed to do that unless he'd actually carried the stuff out of the house himself. And he volunteered. He volunteered to carry my garbage! Do you believe that?"

"This is what everybody thinks they want a piece of," said Hal, a little somberly. "Fame . . ."

"It's overrated," George said. "It means you can't go to a convenience store and let someone see you buy a six-pack of beer. If you do, they either declare you a closet alcoholic, or else the next morning some guy from the beer company turns up on your doorstep asking you to appear in commercials."

"Or both," Mike said.

George looked wry. "Don't laugh. I could be rich about six times over, just now, just out of what I've been offered for endorsements. But I don't want to do that! We're an amateur organization, for one thing. Spat for me is about getting together with my friends, having a good workout, playing together skillfully, and being social afterward. . . . But the problem's a lot worse than that. If I ever get stinking rich, I want it to be from something *I* made, something *I* did. Not something *they* did to me, or for me, as an accidental outgrowth of a pastime, a game, yes, a *game*!—which by itself isn't *worth* that kind of money. But they don't understand that," said George. "And frankly, neither do my family, or my friends, a lot of them . . . They think I'm crazy. And the trouble is, I'm beginning to understand why."

He let out a long breath and had some more iced tea. Catie looked at the glass, and looked at the window, wondering whether George's choice of beverage had anything to do with a possible fear of distant cameras, trained on him, just waiting to see him do something that someone somewhere might consider inappropriate.

"But enough of my troubles," George said at last, and put the glass down. "How about the game?"

"It was super," her brother said. And that was about the last chance Catie would have had to get a word in edgewise for the better part of three quarters of an hour, for the ensuing torrent of spatball jargon took nearly that long to die out, as play after play was taken apart, turned inside out and upside down, analyzed, criticized, and dropped for the consideration of the next one. Mike was an eager participant in this, and Hal gave him a run for his money, while Catie listened with somewhat pained interest to terminology that kept getting tangled up in chords and lunes and great circles and geodesic slams and incidence relations. She sighed at those, for Catie had finished the usual run-in with solid geometry in school last year, and had come away from it successfully, but only just. Afterward, for her, the phrase "Through point A draw a line B" would normally have made a good start for a horrorcast.

But the game itself had been won against an opponent that had widely been expected to dump South Florida unceremoniously out of the tournament. That was the main thing. Now the publicity was heating up, and Hal and Mike amused themselves briefly with reciting some of the more specious and empty-headed rationalizations they had heard in the media for the Banana Slugs' win, everything from plain dumb luck to sunspots. George mostly kept quiet during this, attempting to do something about the second half of his sandwich. Catie had already decided to take hers home in a doggie bag and have another run at it around dinnertime. And possibly a third attempt at breakfast tomorrow . . .

"Your team's been attracting a whole lot more attention than you ever thought you would, I bet," Catie said.

"Yes," George said, putting the sandwich down again with a sigh. "We have. Not all of it friendly."

There was something about the way he said this that made her look at him closely. George was looking out the window again, and his expression was very much that of a man who was sure that someone was watching him.

He glanced back at her. "We're absolutely not supposed to be here, you know," George said after a moment. "It's surprising how easily people get upset when somehow a long-established status quo shifts. Not that publicity won't do the team good in the long run. No matter what happens in these play-offs, our organizational life will be a little easier in the long run. You know—a few less cake sales, a little more time to actually play. But the hostility and confusion surrounding us at the moment are a little sad to see. There are plainly people who genuinely see us as a disruptive influence to the sport, or an embarrassing accident that the sport is going to have to recover from, or a way to make the rest of the sport look bad while we still get a whole lot of money and hold the 'moral high ground' . . . wherever that is for spatball." George let out a long breath that bespoke a fair amount of frustration and anger, all shut down to its lowest possible level for the moment. "It's like they can't understand our right to do what our group formed itself to do: play spat competitively, but never lose sight of the basic pleasures of it just for the sake of the win, or what comes with the win. Flight . . ." For a moment there was a spark of delight in his eyes, and everything was all just that simple. "We're every kid who ever jumped off the couch with a towel tied around his neck, pretending to be a superhero, or boinged along the ground pretending to be Neil Armstrong, or John Glenn, mostly free of gravity, but still free to be human, and to play." He grinned, just briefly. "To play hard, but play fair, too, and be friends again afterward . . ."

Catie nodded quietly for a moment. That kind of feeling was the reason she played soccer, and why she had stayed with the same team of kids from Bradford Academy and the general D.C. area, even when she had opportunity to move to a better team. Sportsmanship, and companionship, expressed through the sport itself and the aftermath, mattered. She raised her eyebrows, then. "Somehow," Catie said, "I don't think that aspect of it is something you've said a whole lot about to the media lately."

"I tried once or twice," said George. "One guy asked me who wrote my speech. Another of the interviewers wanted to know, was I thinking about running for office?" The flicker in George's eyes this time was not a happy one. "I don't talk that way to reporters anymore. Competitiveness, ruthless competitiveness, that they understand. But *joy* . . . ?" He trailed off, shaking his head.

Catie made a wry face. "Trying to teach a pig to read," she said, "wastes your time, and only annoys the pig."

George burst out laughing, and Mike and Hal both looked at him.

"What was that punch line again?" Mike said. "I missed it."

"Nothing," George and Catie said, more or less in unison.

Catie was immensely relieved when Wendy arrived to ask who wanted dessert. Hal, as always, was game. Catie often wondered where he put all the calories he ingested in a day, and how he always failed to show any sign of them afterward. For herself, she passed, content to finish her soda, and George and Mike asked for coffee.

"What time's the press conference?" said Mike, making

the writing-on-a-notepad gesture to Wendy when she came with their coffees.

"Two-thirty," George said. "We'll all stand around in the lobby of their headquarters, trying to look like we really want to be there. They'll have 'real' jerseys there for us to wear, to illustrate what the virtual ones are going to look like." He gave Catie an amused look. "Whether they'll fit anything like as well as the virtual ones is another question. And then there'll be another grilling from the media people, under those hot lights . . . and then we'll have to go virtual and do it again. A couple of hours' worth of interviews, at least, when we should all be in the cubic, practicing. And then back on the plane and home again. . . ."

"But can't you just play the game from up here?" Hal said, surprised. "The sponsor must have Net facilities you can use!"

"They probably have a lot better ones than anything the team has," George said, nabbing the bill from the newly returned Wendy before anyone else had a chance at it, "but I don't care about that, and neither does the team. When we're playing, we all prefer our own Net setups at home. It takes valuable time to get used to someone else's rig, and you never feel quite comfortable . . . and what happens if something goes wrong with it in mid-game? If your own Net machine malfunctions, that's one thing, and maybe you'll know what to do about it. Get up and kick it, or jiggle the phone cable, or whatever. But play a tournament-level game in a strange building, using a strange new machine? No, thanks. I'll admit the extra travel time is a nuisance, but if it gets us home before midnight, that's going to be good enough for me and the rest of the team. We'll manage."

Catie thought she could see his point. George fished around in his pockets and came up with an ElectroWallet card, handed it to Wendy. "Please take ten," he said, and she went away smiling even harder than she had been, which Catie would have thought impossible.

George looked over at Hal. "So have you got your 'seats' sorted out for the game tomorrow?" he said.

"Yup . . . took care of it yesterday."

"Not a bad idea," George said. "The reservations computers have been having trouble with last-minute bookings, the last game or so, they tell me. But do you want to swap your seats for positions in friends-and-family space, down close to the heart of things? We've got room."

Hal was delighted. "Can we really?"

George glanced at Catie. "No problem. Suit you?"

"Suits me fine," she said. "I always like a close look at a winning team."

"Then it's settled. When you're online this evening, check the team server and give it your seat locations. It'll make the swap. Look, I'm sorry we have to go, but the new sponsor would get pretty cranky if the captain was late for the big press push. And if I know these guys, they're going to want some time privately with us before the public part of the proceedings." George got up.

They all headed for the door, where George was handed his ElectroWallet by Wendy. There was a little crowd of the diner staff all waiting there with her by the door to shake George's hand, and as they went out to the street, Hal muttered to Catie, "We ought to come back here later in the week and see if the service is still this good."

She smiled slightly as Mike said his good-byes and headed for his car. He would be driving George to the press conference.

"Listen," said George, shaking Hal's hand, "it's been good meeting you." To Catie, as he shook her hand, he said, "I really enjoyed this. Stay in touch."

"Sure." She smiled politely enough, while at the same time thinking, *I bet you say that to all the*—

"I mean it," George said, and once more there was something about the way he said it that brought Catie up short. It was not exactly urgency in his voice—but at the same time, she couldn't get a handle on just what it *was*.

"Look, wait a second," George was saying. He fumbled around in his pocket and came up with a business card, one of the kind with a Net-readable chip embedded in it: you dropped it onto your Net machine's reading pad, if your machine had one, and it read the embedded address automatically. Or you could always simply read it into your machine off the card.

"Here's my Net address," George said. "It's always nice to run into someone who likes the sport for itself, and isn't blinded by the surrounding hype. If you have time, I wouldn't mind chatting with you occasionally. Or alternately, having the occasional game of chess. I don't have time for tournament play, heck, I don't have time now for proper meals, most days . . . but move-by-move would be fun."

Catie looked at his card, looked at him. "Sure," she said. "Any time."

George waved a little salute at them and headed off toward Mike's car, got in. The two of them drove off. Catie and Hal walked in the other direction, toward the GWU tram station, and found the tram that would head toward home waiting there on layover. They climbed on, and Catie sat down, feeling strangely weary, and yet aware of something at the back of her mind that was poking her for attention, trying to find a way to explain itself and not yet succeeding.

Hal, though, was shaking his head, looking astonished. "Am I completely out of my mind," he said as the tram started up, turning out of the layover loop and into traffic, "or was he making a dive at you?"

Catie reached into her pocket, took out George's card again, glanced at it. "I don't think so," she said after a moment. "I think something else may be going on. He might just want someone to talk to who doesn't automatically see him as a spatball player, or a media figure . . ."

"Or a serious hunk."

"I don't know," Catie said.

What she did know, though, was that as soon as she finished up whatever else her mom wanted her to take care of around the house, she was going to go have a talk with Mark Gridley.

4

Why, when you needed to talk to somebody, was it always so hard to find him? Mark was online so much of the time Catie sometimes wondered how he got enough sleep and sufficient calories for fuel. But when Catie got online that evening and sent a call to Mark's space, all she got was an image of Mark standing by himself, spotlit in the darkness, saying, "I'm either not online right now, or I can't talk . . . so leave me a message, okay?"

And so she did. But the other thing she found, around noon on Sunday—for she got involved in a long debrief with some of her soccer buddies over the game they had played on Saturday afternoon, after the "celebrity lunch"— was in her workspace, in the middle of Catie's mock-up of the Great Hall of the Library of Congress, when she went in to tidy things up before going off to watch the South Florida–Chicago–Moscow Spartak game. It was a simple text message in a window, just hanging there and glowing in the early afternoon light, and it read:

1   P-K4   —

Catie just stood there, smiling slightly, when she saw it. Pawn to King Four. It was the first move of a chess game—the traditional first move, unless you were feeling iconoclastic. She regarded it for a moment. Hal's question came back to her: *Is he taking a dive at you, or what?*

Catie didn't think so. It didn't feel that way, somehow. Granted, it tickled her a little that she was being paid the kind of attention by George Brickner that (if the *People* virtfeature was anything to go by) a significant portion of the girls her age on the continent wished he would pay to *them*. But at the same time she couldn't get rid of the feeling that something else was going on.

I'm going to enjoy finding out what it is, she thought. *But in the meantime . . .*

"Space," she said.

"Have we been introduced?" said her workspace manager.

Mark, Catie thought for about the thirtieth time that week, *we are definitely going to have words about this*. Yet at the same time, she had to admit that there was nothing wrong with the way her manager was functioning. Was it even responding a little faster, a little more flexibly, than it had done before Mark had worked on it? "Just a little heuresis," he had said. If he'd actually improved the way the machine handled input, making it act more intelligently, maybe the tradeoff in smart remarks was worth it, in the long run.

"I sure hope we have, because I want to redecorate a little," Catie said.

"About time," said her workspace in a fussy voice. "Dusting this place just eats up my days."

Catie rolled her eyes. "Never mind that. I want a chessboard in the middle of the floor here."

A regulation tournament-size chessboard with the standard Staunton pieces arrayed on it duly appeared at her feet.

Catie looked up into the empty air of the Great Hall, toward the "place" where she routinely conceived of the workspace management program as "living." *Did I say it was being more flexible?* "That's not what I meant."

"Then you should say what you mean, O Mighty Mistress."

Well, precision was everything, in art and programming both. The miserable program had a point there, though she wasn't going to admit as much out loud.

"Right," Catie said. "Overlay a mosaic representing a chessboard on the mosaics already here. Inset it into the existing floor. I don't want it sticking up over the present design. The size of the chessboard should be three meters by three meters. Make the squares brown and cream to match the colors of the marble in the pillars. And make me some giant pieces to go with it."

The mosaic under her feet obediently wiped itself clean. The chessboard, worked in matching mosaic tiles and the colors she had specified, appeared beneath her feet. And then Catie was completely surrounded by chess pieces twenty feet tall, so that she couldn't stir to right or left, hemmed in as she was by chocolate-brown rooks and knights and bishops.

"Not THAT giant!" she hollered.

"You didn't say," the workspace manager replied calmly.

"I'm going to trade you in for a pocket calculator with a liquid-crystal display," Catie said, "and then I'm going to reprogram *that* with a rock. Make the queen two feet high, and scale all the rest of the pieces accordingly, and hurry up!"

"To hear is to obey, O Sovereign of the Age," said the management program. A blink later all the pieces were of a size to fit the chessboard on the floor.

Catie went over to pick up the brown queen and a few other pieces.

"Don't you want me to set them up for you?" the workspace manager said sweetly.

"No. You just go dust something."

There was quiet for the next few minutes while Catie set up the pieces, both white and brown. Then she moved white's pawn out four spaces in front of his king, and stepped off to one side to look at the board and decide how to respond. She could get flashy and try something like the Ruy Lopez opening, or she could just plod along in her own style, without trying to show off. Finally she decided on the second course of action. George would find out soon enough what Catie was made of without her having to drag any dead chess masters into it.

"I want you to record the moves in the usual notation," Catie said as she picked up her own pawn and moved it out to K4, head-to-head with George's.

The air over the board shimmered, and Catie found herself looking at a pattern of glowing footsteps hanging there, with various curves and arrows hanging between them.

"Not *dance* notation, you idiot lump of silicon!" Catie yelled. "*Chess* notation!"

The window in the air changed to show:

1	P-K4
2	P-K4

"Thank you so much," Catie muttered. "Virtmail George that move, please, and alert me if I'm online when one comes in from him."

"No problem. Do you want out-of-Net paging for moves?"

"No, it's all right. Has Mark Gridley come back in yet?"

"His system still has him flagged as unavailable."

Great, Catie thought. *Well . . . it can keep a day, I suppose. He was the one who was so urgent about wanting to hear about George Brickner. If he's not onsite when I've finally managed it, well, tough.*

But that felt so cold. She sat there wondering. "He said he might run into me at the play-offs," Catie mused. "Space, check the ISF server and find out if Mark has a seat booked for the game this afternoon."

"That information is not available because of privacy issues," her workspace said.

It wouldn't be, would it. . . . She sighed.

At that point a huge voice came echoing into the Great Hall. "Catie!"

She sighed again. "Hal," she said, "lose the visiting wizard act and tell me what you want."

A large image of her brother's head appeared in the air,

surrounded by billows of flame that swirled and brightened around him when he spoke. "I don't know, I kinda like it."

"It'd look even better if you were bald," Catie said, "but I guess I have to wait a few decades for that. What *is* it, runt?"

"Pregame show's starting."

"Yeah, I know. I was going to experience it from the friends-and-family space."

"Oh. Yeah, that's a thought, isn't it! Okay, let's—"

"*Not* until you empty the dishwasher, young man," said another voice from the outside world, not sounding at all like an apparition from Oz, and not needing to. "And then there's the small matter of the laundry piling up in your room."

"But, Dad—!"

Catie tried to keep herself from grinning, and simply couldn't.

"Sorry, Son, you blew it. You've had two days to clean up in there, and knowing you, you'll plead homework tomorrow if we let it go on that long."

"But, Dad, the game—!"

"The sooner you finish this stuff that's been staring at you since four P.M. on Friday, the sooner you'll see what the Slugs do. Get on it."

And silence fell.

"Space, honey," Catie said.

"She wants a favor, I can tell."

Catie was so amused that she didn't much care what her workspace said. "Open a gateway to the friends-and-family space on the ISF server," she said. "And run the usual leave-a-message message if anyone calls for me. I won't be back for a few hours."

"The Great Programmer be praised," said her workspace, "I can finally get some reading done." A doorway opened in the air of her space, and through it, faintly, Catie could hear the roar of the crowd. She stepped through and waved the doorway closed behind her.

• • •

Two hours later she could hardly breathe. The roar, which had been like the distant sea earlier, had hardly stopped for the whole time she'd been in here, even between the halves. Now the clock was running down toward the end of the third half, there was nothing but a tangle of bodies showing in the middle of the volume, and amid shrieks of excitement and outrage from the crowd, the goal hexes had just shifted again, for the third time in no more than five minutes. It was a standard increased-rotation simulation, for such things had happened often enough during the "classic" games played in real microgravity, when the needs of some experiment in the outer ring for increased gravity had caused the whole sphere to be rotated faster. Nominally the computer had charge of such events, inflicting them randomly on the players. But at times like this, when there were three teams at full strength in the cubic, all trying to get control of the ball, they produced the maximum possible confusion. The ball wouldn't go where the players wanted it to. None of them seemed to be able to get that vital, instinctive "extra jump ahead" of the program—

The volume was a mob scene, a whirl of three sets of colors—the yellow and black of South Florida, the red of Chicago, the blue, red, and white of Spartak Moscow. Spartak had possession, its forwards passing the ball down a great-circle curve around the perimeter of the other teams' people; but the crowded center-volume configuration of the last few seconds was already breaking, Melendez and Dawson for South Florida arrowing along toward the live goal that was nearest the end of the great-circle pass corridor that Moscow was using. Spartak had given up on subtlety and was trying for speed, but the belated decision was doing it no good. Chicago, one goal behind South Florida at the moment, was at the same time not beyond simply making sure that it not only scored against South Florida, but kept Spartak from scoring against anybody else under any circumstances—a three-way draw would mean a decrease in its overall "points" total for the tournament, and regardless of the number of games won or drawn, even one point too few could make the difference between winning or losing the tournament if the final games were still tied at the end of penalty or injury time. An extra point in another team's plus column could mean that your own team won on goals but lost on points . . . and at the end of the day, it was the points that would matter. Chicago might get no more points itself today, but it was going to make sure at all costs that Spartak didn't, either.

The goals now precessed one hex along, and everything changed, the previous scrum dissolving into a new one, oriented in a slightly different direction, as the teams reacted to the shift. As usual there were a few seconds during which none of the teams reacted as a whole, but only fragmentarily, shouting orders and suggestions at each other that were nearly lost in the clamor of the crowd. Darien for Chicago nabbed possession of the ball as it was being passed between two Spartak forwards, worked herself out of the tangle of bodies and passed to her fellow forward, Daystrom, who caught the ball in the crook of an elbow and spun in place, in roll axis, looking for the teammate to take the next pass. Most of the other Chicago players were still tangled up on the far side of the scrum, and Daystrom shouted himself hoarse at them to detach themselves and put some air between themselves and the "traffic jam" in the middle of the volume. One or two of them heard and pushed free, but the rest were trying to block either Spartak or South Florida players, and took a moment to respond to Daystrom. Daystrom glimpsed a face that looked ready, Ferguson's, and flung the ball at him—

A leg thrust out of the scrum and kneed around the ball, capturing it. A moment later the body belonging to the ball worked its way out of the scrum and folded itself up double to spin. It was Spartak's Yashenko. A great howl of delight went up from the Moscow fans and the scrum abruptly disintegrated, players scattering in all directions, looking to see where the ball was, locating it, targeting Yashenko and pushing off the volume walls or each other to get at him, to block or tackle.

The movement in the volume became frantic. Yashenko

kept spinning, and one of his teammates, Talievna, was the first to reach him of the multiple "launches" that were heading his way. Within a meter of him she curled up to offer him inertial mass, and Yashenko pushed off against her and was halfway across the spat volume by the time the people who had been coming at him to tackle or block had arrived at his former position.

In an instant it became apparent that he was lining up for an attack on the Chicago goal, at right angles to the Spartak goal directly ahead of him. But there were too many of the Chi players on the wrong side of the volume to defend properly, now, and even the Chi goalie Bonner had been caught away from his post and was now trying to get at the wall for a push in the right direction. The crowd went up in a great howl of excitement as people reacted to the fragmentation among the teams and the prospect of the score, as Yashenko got ready to pass. But there was one place where confusion did not reign quite supreme. Among the bodies now swarming toward the Chicago goal, George Brickner curled himself down into cannonball—possibly inevitable in the confusion, but at least one player was ready for it—then Brickner pushed sideways off Chicago's Daystrom and thus opened up a space between them with the equal-and-opposite reaction. There were shouts of confusion, some from his teammates, but he had seen what they hadn't, and Melendez had seen his glance. As Yashenko headered the ball at Galitsin for the goal, Melendez braced himself off Galitsin and pushed—and the ball flew with terrible speed past Galitsin, who reached for it but couldn't stop it, and smacked squarely into the goal outlined in red, white, and blue before it could precess.

There was a roar of rage and disappointment from the Spartak fans as the computer held the ball in place and did a retrace of recent motions to see who picked up the point. But the referee had seen that perfectly well. "Own goal, Moscow," the referee said over the roar, "credit to South Florida—!"

Another roar, but this time of joy, from the South Florida fans. The rest of the audience was waiting in breathless hope or anguish for the computer to finish the traceback and agree or disagree with the ref, but the digits on the scoreboard hexes embedded in the transparent walls of the spat volume burned briefly bright . . . and then changed from 2–1–1 to 2–2–1.

Play resumed, and if it had been fast before, it was furious now. Twenty-one men and women, angry or wildly excited or both, jostled for control of the ball as it was fired back into the volume. It vanished into a flying scrum of bodies wearing yellow and red about half and half, while the ones in red, white, and blue changed tactics, as was possibly understandable, and simply tried to keep either of the others from scoring. This was one of those situations in which spatball started to more closely resemble a particularly spiteful playground game of keep-away than anything else. Somehow, though, Chicago managed to get hold of the ball again, and another hand-around began as Hanrahan emerged from the scrum with the ball gripped desperately behind one bent knee. He did a 180-degree somersault in the pitch axis and flung the ball away again, revealing (to Moscow if no one else) that the pass he had been setting up was a feint, and that three of his teammates were lining up in great-circle on South Florida's goal. But it was too late. The crowd was already counting down, and there was no injury time, and even as Jarvik took the pass from Hanrahan and fired it at Torrance, who in turn fired it at the goal, the South Florida goalie was there, out of nowhere, wrapping herself around the ball like an oyster around somebody's escaped pearl.

"Houdini!" the South Florida fans screamed at the goalie in tribute, but Zermann paid no attention to them—opening herself up again, glancing around her for no more than a second, and fisting the ball away sideways like a bolt of orange lightning at Brickner, who caught it in his elbow and tightened in for spin—

And the horn went. Catie jumped up and flung her arms around Zermann's brother Kerry, who had been sitting beside her rigid as a statue for the last fifteen minutes, but now was jumping up and down and screaming "Slugs!

Slugs!" like everyone else within the twenty-meter diameter that circumscribed the Slugs friends-and-family
area. From behind her, Hal caromed into Catie, and she
dropped Kerry Zermann and pounded her brother's head
in sisterly delight. All around them the crowd of sixty
thousand was in bedlam, and in the spat volume team
members of all kinds were hugging each another and jerseys were being pulled off and sent sailing across the volume to other players, who slipped them on and came
across to shake hands, some cheerfully, some with scowls.
The announcer was shouting into the main sound link,
"—and South Florida and Chicago tie, two-two, with
Moscow Spartak falling by the wayside with an own goal
and only one score during the whole of an *incredible*
game, one that'll go down in the record books for sheer
unpredictability and brilliant play—the umpire congratu-
lating both sides now as the Slugs and the Fire progress
to the quarter-final stage, both teams going into the po-
sitional lottery along with New York, Los Angeles, the
Grasshoppers of Xamax Zurich, Manchester United High,
Rio de Janeiro, and Sydney Gold Stripe. A game that will
go down in spat history for possibly the latest . . ."

Catie found herself wondering later, *The latest what*?—
for when things quieted down again enough for her to
notice things, she was in the "locker room" with the Slugs,
their entourage, and about fifty other people, mostly from
the sports networks. The locker room wasn't any such
thing, of course, any more than it had to be in any other
virtual sport. The players' actual bodies were mostly in
their own homes, and if they needed showers, or someplace to change their clothes, such things were only steps
away from their own implant chairs. But the need for a
place to celebrate after a won game, and to deal with the
press, still existed, and so here they all were, the Slugs
laughing, shouting, jubilant even after only achieving a
draw. At first Catie tried to keep herself calm in the midst
of all this, but it was just silly. So much excitement, so
tightly concentrated, simply overwhelmed your senses—
the reporters running around sticking virtual mikes (rep-
resentative of link-out programs to their own broadcast-

ers' servers) into people's faces, the champagne being squirted around with total abandon—for when the session finally broke up, no one would actually be sticky, and no money for the bubbly stuff would actually have been wasted—the hoots and shouts of victory, the jokes and jibes, and the big stuffed banana slug being paraded around the locker room, with some team members and hangers-on bowing to it ceremoniously, and others following it around in an impromptu conga line—Catie couldn't help but laugh, especially when George's co-captain, Mark, left one interview with the CNNSI reporter and came up to her with what looked like a very big peanut butter jar wrapped in prismatic gift paper. He was holding the lid on, and he said to Catie, in a mysterious voice, "Want a look?"

"Sure," Catie said.

He opened the lid. She peered in. Then she raised her eyebrows and said, "I thought they were bigger."

"Aww," Mark said, sounding disappointed. Plainly he had been expecting a more emphatic response. "And you looked like such a sweet, innocent little thing, too."

Catie grinned. "Guilty on one count, maybe. But when you've had as many weird things put down your back by your little brother as I have over the last seventeen years, one slug more or less doesn't matter much. Besides, I think that one's asleep."

"Asleep? How can you tell?" Mark stared into the jar. "Listen, seriously, how can you—?" But at that point one of the reporters from AB/NBC came up to Mark with a "mike" and started asking him questions about Chicago's "front five," and Catie slipped away, grinning. That response had paralyzed her brother, too, a few years ago, and had won her at least an hour of peace somewhere along the line.

Very slowly the locker room began to clear out, and as it did, George Brickner drifted over toward Catie, glancing around him with an expression that overtly looked like satisfaction. But there was still something else going on too, that uncertain quality in his gaze that Catie had noticed before and had not been able to put a name to. Seeing it again now, it began to bother her more than ever. If there was a form of art she preferred above all others, it was portraiture, and after a lot of studying of faces, over time, she was beginning to get a sense of whether the face in question was (for lack of a better phrase) comfortable with itself. George's face was not, and Catie kept wondering why.

"Well," he said, watching one last reporter getting into Melendez's face again, "at least that's over. Now we start getting ready to go into the lottery."

Catie raised her eyebrows at that. "You're going to have to coach me here a little, George . . . I'm still new to this game. Though I think I heard some of the reporters going on about this earlier."

"Oh. Well, at the quarterfinal level, the teams that have 'survived' that long go into a lottery to determine who plays who in what order. Originally, it was a way of avoiding accusations that one team or another was using undue influence to have first crack at the spat volume on the Space Station." He waved away one of his teammates who was coming at him and Catie with one more champagne bottle. "Pete, why don't you drink some of the stuff? Nice vintage, no calories!"

The answer was a rude noise, after which Dalton departed to squirt someone else. ". . . Anyway, later they kept the same routine to make sure that time slots in the dedicated 'sealed' server were distributed fairly, since the security protocols in the single server only allow one game to be played at a time. A spat tournament isn't something you can stage over multiple venues, like a real-world sport. At least it couldn't be done so far. That may change now. With money pouring into the sport the way it has been, they'll be able to afford to set up and maintain at least one more dedicated server, maybe two. One of the good things that'll come of all this sponsorship, I hope, eventually."

George sighed then. "At least the hardware upgrades will be good if the software is improved . . . the stuff we have is already getting kind of clunky. In particular, there are problems handling the larger 'crowds.' That's an increasingly thorny issue, and it's going to get worse as the virtual 'gate' gets bigger and more and more people are attracted to the sport."

"Don't tell me that you're longing for the good old days when spat was smaller, and only a few aficionados would turn up. . . ." This was something that Catie had heard from at least one of the commentators over the past couple of weeks.

George laughed at her. "Are you kidding? This time, right now, is going to be looked back on in twenty years as spat's golden age. I like it the way it is." Then his face clouded. "I'd like it better still, though, if we'd won today. We should have."

"But you didn't."

George looked at her sharply. "You don't understand me," George said. "I wasn't saying, 'I wish we'd won.' I was saying, 'We *should* have won.' " He looked at Catie to see if she was getting what he was saying, and he lowered his voice. "Especially in the second half. The force we applied to the ball, the way we were handling it, should have produced a certain given result then . . . and it didn't. Something was wrong in there. I felt it again in the third half . . . which was why I was insisting on so much contact, and only shooting at goal from up close."

Catie understood him, and what he was saying unnerved her. "You're saying that the feel of the virtual spat space, the way it was behaving, had been interfered with somehow."

He nodded.

Catie shook her head. "I know there are games where that happens on purpose. The way a golf greenskeeper can alter the 'lie' of the greens to make a hole harder to play . . . or the groomers at a bowling alley can varnish or wax the alleys to make the ball behave one way or another. It even happens in baseball . . . the guys who mow the lawn do the infield to favor their team's hitting tendencies."

"That's legal, within limits, and for those games. But in spat the server is maintained by a central authority, not by the individual teams, and the spat volume's behavior is supposed to be neutral."

"So to change the way the scoring surface was acting . . . it would mean that someone had to tamper with the server," Catie said, also keeping her voice low. "But that's supposed to be impossible. The servers are sealed, aren't they?"

"They're supposed to be," said George. "But exactly what that means in operational terms, I haven't the slightest idea. Do you?"

Catie didn't, but she resolved to find out, and she knew someone who could make the issue as clear to her as it needed to be. "No," she said. "Not at the moment."

George nodded. Catie looked at him and got the clear sense that he knew more about what she was up to than he was letting on, but he was being cagey about it. Maybe he was wise . . . for there was always the possibility, in any virtual encounter, that one was being listened to. Even encryption was not always everything it was cracked up to be. For some of the more routine forms of encryption, the "soft" ones, various law enforcement organizations held back-door keys . . . and not even law enforcement, Catie knew, was immune to occasionally being compromised. When you came right down to it, even law enforcement officers were just people, and people, however regrettably, had weaknesses that could occasionally be exploited by those with the inclination to do so.

"Tell me how it felt to you," Catie said after a moment.

"Like the ball was bouncing wrong," George said. "As if the virtual 'rotation speed' of the spat space had been altered without warning. Not a whole lot. But when you work in microgravity for long enough, you get to know the feel. We've had astronauts in to check it for 'reality,' and they've always said it was right on."

Catie nodded again. "Meanwhile," she said, "did you get my move?"

"Just pregame." George gave her an amused look. "Conservative."

"If you can tell that much about me from just one move," Catie said, "you're pretty good."

"That's what they tell me," George said, and gave her a superior look, which he couldn't hold—a moment later he was laughing.

"When's the lottery?" Catie said.

"Tuesday evening," George said. "Usually it's not a big deal . . . but I hear it's going prime time this year." He was still smiling, but once again that expression of guarded concern was in his eyes.

Catie looked across the room at Hal, who had recovered quite nicely from his late arrival at the game, and was now gazing down into Mark's jar with interest. A second later he took it from Mark and headed in Catie's direction. Time to put on her game face. . . . "When you send your next move along," she said, "I'll get in touch, and we can have a little chat."

George nodded. "I'll look forward to that."

"Cates," Hal was saying, "how can you *tell* it's asleep?"

Catie smiled.

Elsewhere, in a virtual bar far away, it was no longer afternoon, but night; and two shadowy forms sat on either side of a marble table, under the blue-tinged mood lighting, and eyed one another coolly.

"Lucky for you they drew," Darjan said.

Heming kept himself still, and didn't gulp . . . though he felt like it. Chicago's draw had been entirely too tight a thing. "I can't understand why they didn't win," he said.

Darjan gave him a dry look. "Maybe our principals' enthusiasm is misplaced," he said. "The team was given the equivalent of nearly half an hour's worth of free goals. They weren't able to make any decent use of the time. Whatever that may suggest to *us*, it's suggesting other things to the people who're most interested in what they do next. We're going to have to look at more robust forms of intervention."

"Still, they got into the play-off pool anyway," said Heming after a moment. "The draw is Tuesday. The odds of them being matched off against South Florida again are minuscule."

"Forty-four to one is not minuscule," Darjan said quietly. "Two point six billion to one, like a respectable lottery, the same chance you have to be hit by a meteorite, now *that's* minuscule. Forty-four to one is too damn good. And no matter who South Florida plays, their odds are *still* too damn good. This has got to be sorted out, Heming. Fast. What are you doing about it?"

Heming didn't quite squirm, though he wanted to. "Some people are going to go have a look at the South Florida team members' Net machines," he said. " 'Routine maintenance.' "

Darjan sat quiet for a moment. "That sounds like a thought," he said finally. "As long as you're not planning anything so infantile as having the machines fail in the middle of a game."

Heming looked briefly horrified. "Uh, of course not. Little changes, though, in the programming of each. Installation of conditionals."

Darjan was silent for a moment. "That might work," he said. "As long as deinstallation procedures are included as well. Be a shame if someone went looking at their Net machines' routines, after the fact, and found something out of the ordinary there."

"Of course deinstalls will be put in at the same time," Heming said. "There are ways to do such things that won't alarm the usual antiviral and system-scan diagnostics. It's all taken care of."

"Then get on with it," Darjan growled. "The first game is Thursday . . . and it had better go the way our principals want, if South Florida is involved . . . or they're going to start taking your intervention, or lack of it, personally."

This time Heming *did* gulp, whether he wanted to or not.

Monday afternoon Catie got in from school and went online again to clean up her virtmail, and to make another attempt to get in touch with Mark. It wasn't like him to be incommunicado for so long, except for his actual school time. He seemed to practically live online, and Catie thought that the only reason he didn't get in trouble over this was probably that his parents had to spend so much of their time online as well. She stood there in the Great Hall of her workspace and said, "Still nothing from him?"

"Nothing. Should we call the media and tell them the engagement's off, boss?"

"Fff," Catie said, a soft sound of annoyance, but it wasn't serious—she had other things on her mind. *I wonder if he's had to go away suddenly with his dad or something. They do travel a lot—*

She plopped down into her beat-up comfy chair and brooded for a few moments. *Well, no point in worrying about this any more until I hear from him,* she thought. *If I—*

"Incoming call," said her workspace manager. "Requesting entry into the space, if you're available."

"Who is it?"

"James Winters."

Catie's mouth fell open, and she stood up hurriedly. Every member of the Net Force Explorers knew James Winters by sight. He was the group's liaison to Net Force as a whole, and theoretically on call to anyone in the Explorers if they had some problem. That was the theory, anyway. Every Explorer also knew perfectly well that Winters had other work in Net Force which was far more important than his liaison work, and that it would be stupid to bother him with things that weren't genuinely crucial. More than stupid: suicidal, at least to your employment prospects at Net Force, if you seriously intended ever to work there . . . for James Winters was unquestionably going to be one of the committee that decided whether you got hired, and if you had ever wasted his time on purpose, he would certainly remember.

When he came looking for you, however . . . all bets were off. "Let him right in," Catie said.

A doorway formed in the air, dark at first, then revealing a rather standard-looking government office with afternoon sunlight coming into it through the stripe-shadows of Venetian blinds, and through the door stepped James Winters. About six feet tall, broad-shouldered, with a Marine brush cut and a thoughtful, chiseled face, Winters stood there in conservative street clothes—cream short-sleeved shirt, dark trousers—and looked up and around him with recognition and (Catie thought) some pleasure. "Afternoon, Catie," he said.

"Good afternoon!" she said, trying not to sound too strangled as she said it.

He turned around to look at the frescoed ceilings of the Great Hall, and the carved marble pillars. "Nice job. Did you do this from scratch?"

"Uh, yes," Catie said. "It's taken a while . . . but I see a lot of the real building."

"Yes, your mother works there, doesn't she," Winters said, continuing to look upward.

"That's right. Can I offer you a seat?" Catie said.

"Thanks, yes."

"Space?"

"One chair coming up," said her workspace management program, and produced an executive-style swivel chair off to one side of the "giant" chessboard. Winters went to it and sat down, glancing at the game as he did so. "I hope I'm not interrupting anything."

"Not at all."

"Good. Let me start out by saying that this has nothing to do with the Net Force Explorers, as such."

"Oh," Catie said. *Boy, that sounded intelligent.*

Winters smiled, a dry expression. "All right," he said. "Catie, I see that you had a meeting with George Brickner the other day."

Catie blinked at that. "Uh, yes. He was in town with his team before the Chicago game." *And Net Force is watching him. How interesting . . .*

"Your brother set that up, I take it."

"Yes, he's buddies with one of George's friends."

"Do you mind if I ask you a question or two about that lunch?"

"No," Catie said carefully. "But I hope you'll tell me why."

Winters gave her a hard, thoughtful look. It wasn't an unfriendly one. "Before we get into detail on that," Winters said, "tell me if I'm up to speed on something.

You've been working in imagery sciences, haven't you? Fine arts mostly, but a fair amount of emphasis on techniques for manipulating virtual spaces."

"That's right," Catie said. "Staying at patina-level isn't much good if you're going to get seriously involved in sampling and analyzing virtual content. You have to go down to structure-level as well. I may not be a code wizard as yet, but I can recognize from an image what's been done to it to make it look the way it does, and what else has to be done to change that, or to restore it if there's been a change."

Winters nodded. One part of Catie's brain was shrieking at her, *Are you out of your mind, you're only seventeen, how can you possibly be making claims like this so calmly to this man?* while another, perfectly at ease, was saying in response, *But they're true.* "False modesty," her father was always telling her, "is potentially more fatal to your career than a bullet in the brain. If you know how to do something, *say* so. You don't have to brag, but you do have to tell yourself the truth about what you know how to do; otherwise you can't make those talents available to others . . . and if you can't do that, what good are those talents to you or anybody else?" . . . Now, Catie thought, she would find out whether her dad was right.

"All right," Winters said. "That particular aspect of your studies is fortuitous at the moment. Let me backtrack a little. You've started following spatball?"

"Yes," Catie said. "My brother got me into it."

"He's been interested for a while?"

"I wouldn't say a *long* while," Catie said, caution overcoming her for the moment. "Some weeks, anyway."

"Ah, I see. . . . So here's what this is about," Winters said. "Net Force has some concerns about the conduct of the upcoming spatball play-offs. Not just because of the presence of South Florida in them. But the Banana Slugs—" He stopped, and grinned. "I'm sorry. It makes me want to laugh every time I use the name. Have you ever *seen* a banana slug?"

"Just yesterday," Catie said. "Several times. At close range."

"I see you're overcome with the excitement. Well, anyway . . . The team's presence in the play-offs is serving to crystallize out various concerns we've had about the conduct of spatball, and some other virtual sports, for a while now. Concerns about the integrity of their gaming environments, for one thing."

That made Catie stop very still for a moment, thinking of what George had said to her . . . and the larger implications of his words. When a sport was played entirely in the virtual realm, it became unusually vulnerable to being disrupted by people with a vested interest in one outcome or another. Normally, as in the case of spatball, there were special committees and organizations set up by the governing bodies of such sports, which assigned officials whose jobs were specifically to keep the virtual sports arenas "clean." The officials made sure that servers remained untampered with, that scoring and monitoring software was working properly and was properly manned and operated during games, things of that sort.

But who watches the watchers? Catie thought. *If your officials are crooked, how are the players, or anyone else, ever going to find out?*

"Environment integrity has been a problem of sorts ever since this branch of sports got started," Winters said. "All the umpires, referees, and invigilators for the various sports routinely undergo random testing. Lie-detector tests, drug testing, all the usual routines. It's not a perfect solution by any means, from the civil rights point of view as well as many others, but it's worked well enough, by and large. However, it's never safe to assume that a system like this is working well enough so that it doesn't need periodic reassessment. When something has become status quo . . . that's the time that people start looking for ways to subvert it without the subversion showing. And we have some evidence that that might be happening now."

He leaned back in his chair. "I don't want to get into too much detail right this moment," Winters said. "Among other reasons, I don't want to take a chance of prejudicing your own ideas, or pushing your judgment in one direction or another. But the indications of interference with spatball have been mounting up over recent months . . . and now South Florida is going to cause some of the forces involved in that interference to start showing their hands. We've been waiting for this for a while."

"I want to get something clear here. You mean," Catie said, "that these 'forces' are involved in actively fixing games."

Winters nodded. "There are always people who gamble," he said. "And the other side of that coin is that there are always people who want to control the gambling, or try to, to make a profit from it. In some cases, like casino gambling, the control is fairly benign. You go in to play mathematical games of chance, with easily predictable odds. Sometimes you win, sometimes you lose, and the house rakes off its ten percent as part of the normal state of affairs. But when gambling starts to try to affect less mathematically predictable games, and affect them a lot more robustly—games with a lot of variables . . ."

"Like sports," Catie said.

"Like sports—then matters can get out of hand. Now, people will always bet. It just seems to be part of human nature, something that can't be wiped out . . . which is why most governments around the world have legitimized at least certain kinds of sports gambling. From the government's point of view, if you can't stamp something out, tax it and attempt to regulate it. But there are always elements that chafe at that control, and who feel that what the government is taxing, they should have a piece of, too. They lay their own bets—sometimes through big syndicates, as a means of spreading the profit around so that it's not too obvious—and then they influence the sports they're betting on in any way they dare, to get as close as they can to the results they want."

"I suppose," Catie said, "that it would annoy these syndicates if there were sports they *couldn't* influence. . . ."

"That's part of what's going on in this particular case, we think," Winters said. "They see it as lost revenue. But also, when they get used to running a racket or a betting pattern in a specific way, and something comes in to upset that pattern, that can annoy the syndicates, too . . . and occasionally they get annoyed enough to stand up on their hind legs and try to do something about it."

Winters got up and began to pace. "At the moment, there are at least two syndicates that we suspect have been interfering, or trying to interfere, with spatball over the last couple of years. They've kept their interventions small-scale, until now. Co-opting a few players, trying to get them to throw games, or to get their teammates to help them do it . . . that kind of thing. It wasn't that successful, as far as we can tell. But even when this didn't work, the syndicates were making enough money from betting on spatball that it wasn't worth making a big stink when things went wrong."

"But then South Florida came along," Catie said, "and changed the pattern."

"That's right. Now, by and large, the syndicates aren't going to go broke just because of South Florida. They don't bet on just one team to win. They use the normal bookmakers' 'spread' to cover their losses. But South Florida *is* disturbing the syndicates' old established pattern. The syndicates we're watching—well, these particular gamblers are very conservative. They hate to have to develop new plans when the old ones have been working just fine. For the sake of getting rid of this new factor in the odds, we think one or the other of the main betting syndicates is moving to try something—we think they may actually try to tamper with the virtual environment itself."

He sat down again, hunched forward a little, his hands folded. "Normally they'd shy away from this," Winters said, "for fear of detection. But if they do this now, and manage to pull it off successfully, then they'll try it again, in other sports . . . and the effects down the road could be very bad. Everything from the various 'fantasy leagues' that play casually around the world to the 'real' leagues that play under virtual conditions could be affected, if we don't get a handle on this and stop it now. We want to catch the perpetrators with their hands in the cookie jar, conclusively. And the rest of the intervention must be complete, leaving no doubt in anyone's mind that we are completely on top of this problem before it really gets going."

Catie sat there quietly thinking for a moment. "So," she said, "it would be good if Net Force actually *was* completely on top of it."

Winters gave Catie a long, level look, and she abruptly broke out in a sweat, wondering if she had gone a little too far. Then the Net Force Explorers liaison cracked a small and appropriately wintry smile, no more than a couple of millimeters' worth and only on one side of his mouth, but enough to relieve Catie of the impression that she was in trouble.

"It takes time to put an operation together," Winters said, "and there are times you concentrate on one aspect of it to the detriment of others. We're trying to remedy that problem right now."

"That's why Mark was asking about meeting George Brickner, wasn't it."

Winters sighed. "Whatever else we might seek to accuse Mark Gridley of in the real world," he said, "subtlety wouldn't be on the list. Well, never mind, he makes up for it elsewhere. Catie, one of our concerns is whether this attempt to fix the ISF play-offs might extend into the personnel of the teams themselves. 'Big sports' are already vulnerable for any number of reasons, and we're looking into all the professional teams involved in the spatball play-offs as a matter of course. Rio, in particular, and Chicago, have some potentially unsavory connections, which have been sliding around just under the surface. But a nonprofessional team like the Banana Slugs is vulnerable in all kinds of other ways. South Florida, as you know, is composed of fairly ordinary people with fairly ordinary jobs—the most exciting employment any of them holds down is probably the K-9 work that the center forward does for the U.S. Customs office at the Port of Miami—and in such a situation, the prospect of a big payoff for doing something that you would almost cer-

tainly never get caught at would tempt most anybody."
He sighed. "Heck, it would even tempt *me* at the pay my
grade pulls, except that I'm widely known to be incor-
ruptible, and besides, I'm sure there's someone taking a
look at my bank account now and then."

"I'm not sure I'd believe that any of the people on that
team would be involved in throwing games," Catie said.
"But I've only known them for a couple of days. . . ."
Then she glanced up. "One thing you should know,
though. When we were having lunch, George Brickner
heard me say that I was in the Net Force Explorers. I
wouldn't say the conversation changed tack after that . . .
but I caught a couple of odd looks from him."

"Odd, how?"

"It's hard to say," Catie said. Indeed, she was still trying to analyze them to her own satisfaction.

"Did he look suspicious of you in some way?"

Catie thought about that. "No," she said. "Whatever
was on his mind, I don't think it was that. I'm still not
sure what he wants, but he's definitely more attracted than
repelled."

"Hmm . . ." Winters brooded for a moment. "Well," he
said, "let's get to why I came to see you. Obviously, I'd
like your help in this operation, if your parents will sanc-
tion you assisting Net Force as we investigate. I have to
add that normally I'm chary of allowing Net Force Explorers to become involved in open cases in any official
way. But your access to George Brickner, in a way that
would stand up to any outside scrutiny, is a gift in this
situation, a gift I'm afraid that I am hoping to utilize. That
aside, however, I would judge the threat to be minimal in
this case at this point . . . and, besides, we already have
another Net Force Explorer involved."

Catie grinned. Winters, seeing the grin, rolled his eyes.

"Yes, well," he said. "Normally we do our best to resist
the urge to use Mark as a stalking horse. It's all too easy
to get in the habit of relying on a talent so close to home,
and it would be exploitative. Mark has a right to a normal
childhood, one that doesn't involve being the tool, willing
or otherwise, of a law enforcement agency." He raised his

eyebrows, a resigned look. "But since Mark seems to routinely and consciously *sabotage* all attempts by his parents to provide him with a normal childhood, we're all aware that mostly this is a losing battle. And anyway, there are occasions when it becomes briefly appropriate to temporarily set our scruples aside."

Catie got up and started to pace a little herself.

"Anyway," Winters said, "will you think about it?"

"I have been thinking about it," she said. "For my own part, the answer's yes. And for George's part . . . I have this idea that he may be asking for help, somehow. Maybe he suspects what's going on. Either way, it sounds like you'd be in a position to help him out."

". . . Yes," said Winters, and he was looking at her thoughtfully. "And so would you. You and he seem to have struck it off pretty positively . . . and he seems willing to talk to you about what's going on."

"Not just willing," said Catie, "but positively eager." That was, in fact, something that had made her wonder a little.

Winters sat quiet for a few moments at that. "All right," he said. "Catie, as the play-offs progress, would you be willing to be a good listener for a while?"

"To find out whether anything illegal is going on inside the club?"

"That would be part of it."

Catie held still for a moment, thinking. She wasn't wild about the idea of being some kind of informer. Yet she thought back to what George himself had been saying about the difficulties of spatball in general, and South Florida in particular.

"I don't want you to be uncomfortable about this," Winter said. "If you feel you can't in good conscience be involved in an operation of this kind, even tangentially, I'll understand. Yet at the same time it's a unique opportunity to make sure that the forces we suspect are moving in on spatball don't get a chance to consolidate a chokehold on the sport at large. The money coming into spat means that all the levels of play, especially the more amateur ones, can funnel their share of the funds into the community projects they love . . . and keep their sport clean and alive in its present form. But a loss to the organized crime people moving in on them now will suggest that the rest of the sport is weak as well, and can be covertly suborned by illegal payments and shady influence. . . ."

Catie stood silent for a few moments. "Mr. Winters," she said. "George is a friend. I'm not going to lead him on. But what he tells me freely—"

"That's all we'd want to hear about," Winters said. "I wouldn't think of asking you to betray any confidences. But any indication that George was uneasy about what was going on inside his team would definitely help us work out how best to keep the damage that we suspect is about to happen, from happening at all. . . ."

He stood up, too. "Obviously you're going to need to talk to your parents about this, and so am I. But there wasn't any point in talking to them until I'd spoken to you first. This isn't likely to be a dangerous business, which is one of the reasons I'm willing to involve you. At the same time, you're going to need to keep your eyes open. We are going to be sniffing around people who are intent on making sure no one finds out what they're doing . . . and when they begin to suspect that that's happening anyway, things are likely to get uncomfortable. That's the point at which you're going to excuse yourself and let the Net Force operatives handle things."

She nodded. "That's fine with me. I'm a quiet type at heart."

He didn't quite snort. "Then what you're doing asking Mark Gridley to do maintenance work on your computer is beyond me," he said. "But we'll leave that aside for the moment. Anyway, when I find out where Mark is, I'll ask him to come talk to you about the 'sealed' game servers, so that you know what kind of things to listen for when you talk to George Brickner. Meanwhile, please talk to your folks soon, Catie. And let me know when you have. I'll be in touch with them shortly thereafter to answer any questions."

"I will, Mr. Winters."

He gave her a wave, then headed back through the door into his office, which sealed behind him.

Catie stood there gazing down at the chessboard and trying to decide what to do next.

5

Eventually she got offline and went looking for her dad. His studio door was open a crack, which meant it was all right for him to be disturbed—"as if I'm not disturbed most of the time" was his usual line, "at least, to judge by what your mother says." Catie pushed the door open a little and found her father standing in the middle of the studio, the CNNSI artwork on its easel pushed off to one side for the moment, while he stood under the spotlight with the digitizing camera on its tripod, apparently changing a lens.

"You busy, Dad?" Catie said.

"Just thinking bad thoughts about Zeiss," he said. "Come on in."

"What's the matter?" She came over and looked curiously at the lenses her father had laid out on the small table nearby, big, black-cased, knurl-edged things.

"Aah, the new lens is still showing chromatic aberration around the edges," he said.

"The one they just sent you as a replacement?"

"Yeah," her father said. He looked with distaste at the lens he was holding in his hand. "There are two possibilities, and neither of them is great. Either the replacement

suffers from the same problem as the original wide angle—which is just possible—or there's something wrong
with the camera. Naturally that's what Zeiss is going to
claim when I send this lens back to them. And the second
camera's in the shop, so I can't test the lens to see if it
fails in the same way." He frowned. "And I need the
wide-angle for this—the other lenses can't get the whole
painting in one shot. And I refuse to waste time trying to
shoot this picture in pieces. It never matches up perfectly,
no matter how hard you try. . . ."

"If you'd done this in virtual space, in Pinxit or one of
the other rendering programs," Catie said, knowing perfectly well what the response was going to be, "you
wouldn't have this problem."

"I hate Pinxit," her father said, with some relish. "Its
user interface is a complete waste of time. And if I'd
never married your mother, I wouldn't have you standing
here making fun of me while I'm going insane in the
name of art, either. So let's not play the If game." He
gave her a rather dry look, but it was still affectionate.
"Meanwhile, did you come in here just to make fun of
my creative genius being stymied, or was there something
else?"

"Uh, yeah." As briefly as she could without leaving out
anything important, Catie described to her father the visit
she had just had from James Winters.

While she was talking, her father plopped himself down
on the paint-spattered couch and sat there turning the of-
fending camera lens over and over in his hands. When
Catie finished, he looked up at her for a few moments and
didn't say anything.

Catie stood there and tried to conceal the fact that she
was twitching slightly.

"And?" her dad said.

"And what?"

"What do you think you should do?"

"I want to help," Catie said.

Her father started turning the lens over in his hands
again. "Your mother's attitude," he said. It was something
of a joke in the family that Catie seemed to take a whole

lot more after her mother than her father. "You think you can make a difference?"

"I think I might be able to," Catie said. "It's worth a try."

Catie's dad raised his eyebrows and gave her a look she couldn't quite decipher. "Is this opinion entirely motivated by the desire for justice and fair play," he said, "or does it have something to do with George?"

Catie flushed. "Naturally it has *something* to do with him," she said, "but, Dad, it's not what I think you're thinking. If you *are* thinking that."

"What," her father said, "that he's a little old for you?"

Now she laughed at him. "Of *course* he's a little old for me. It's not that kind of interest, Dad. Maybe—" The sudden realization brought her up short. "Maybe it's that I feel a little sorry for him."

"Huh . . . ?" Her father looked surprised. "Why? When he's suddenly becoming a national celebrity, and he could be rich if he wanted to? . . . And probably will be, no matter what his intentions are," her father added. "They have a way of getting to you, the sponsors, the big money . . . if they want you. Time is on their side."

Catie filed that thought away for consideration later. "It's more like that he's a little lonely," she said. "He has friends, there's no problem there . . . but I get a feeling that he doesn't discuss the stuff that's going on with the team with them all that much. If he suspects there's a problem, maybe he's afraid of involving them."

"But not afraid of involving *you*," her father said, suddenly sounding a little fierce.

"If I hadn't made it plain I was interested," Catie said, "he wouldn't have taken the issue much further. I'm sure of that."

Her father sat there for a few more moments, turning the lens over in his hands. "Well," he said eventually, "your mom'll be home from the library in a couple of hours . . . she and I will have a talk then." He gave Catie another of those undecipherable looks. "Hold off on talking to George for the time being, okay?"

"Okay," Catie said. "But we're playing chess. If a move comes through—"

Her father allowed a slight smile to emerge. "All right," he said, "deal with that, obviously." He got up. "Meanwhile I have to get on the Net and try to get some satisfaction out of Zeiss, who will doubtless tell me that I'm out of my mind, and why should they replace this optic again. . . ." The smile turned into a very sour grin. " 'Customer service' . . . another of the great implied oxymorons of our time. Go on, honey, scoot out of here."

Catie scooted.

She paused long enough to make herself a tuna sandwich, and while she was making it, considered her options. *I might have to hold off on talking to George for the moment . . . but there's nothing to prevent me talking to Mark Gridley. Assuming I can find the little twerp.*

Catie finished the sandwich and had a Coke, then went off to the family room and sat down in the implant chair, and just vagued out for a moment or so. Her eye fell on the crack in the corner of the room, by the bookcase. *Is that thing getting bigger?* she thought. *Really must mention it to Mom.* Her father might do repairs and so forth around the house, but it was her mother who usually noticed such things needed to be done, and got them organized. She was, in most ways, the silent power in the family. Though Catie's dad might come down hard in one direction or another, he rarely did so without consulting her mother first, except as regarded small things. *And how's she going to take this business with George? I wonder,* Catie thought. Her mom could be unusually protective, sometimes. A little too much so, by Catie's way of thinking. *But then, if as Dad says we're so much alike, it would seem that way to me, I guess. . . .*

Catie sighed and lined up her implant with the Net box, activating it. A moment later she was standing in the Great Hall, looking at her beat-up comfy chair, along with piles of e-mails and art projects that she hadn't yet finished filing. *It'll have to wait.* "Space—" she said.

"What, you again?"

She smiled grimly. "Get me Mark Gridley."

"Checking his space for you now."

She stood there looking at the various pieces of completed and half-completed artwork lying on the floor in their "iconic" forms. *When was the last time I sat down and actually did some art*? Catie thought. She could think of about fifty things that needed to be done to the *Appian Way* piece, especially after the talk she'd had with Noreen the other day. She hadn't even had time to unshell the Luau lighting program—

Her own space suddenly dissolved away to darkness. A second or so later that darkness began to lift again, like a slow dawn, but though the ground under her feet, a dusty, pockmarked surface, began to pale, the "sky" did not.

A moment later Catie saw why. The sky was black, and full of stars that burned, unwinking, unhampered by any breath of atmosphere. The dusty, pale ground was more than just pockmarked. It was scattered with little chunks of rock, something porous and light-looking, like pumice, and the pockmarks weren't just potholes, they were craters. The nearby ones were small, but there were bigger, walled ones further off—ancient impact craters, their insides impossible to see from where Catie stood, though here and there a "splash peak" from some ancient gout of lava caught in the act of recoalescing with its crater's briefly molten bottom still stood up above the rim.

She looked around her, very impressed. Off to her left, nearly new, there was the Earth, a bright, blue-burning crescent, and ever so faintly its dark side, North America and the Pacific mostly, was lit by moonlight, the old Earth in the new Earth's arms. Catie smiled slightly, and finished her turn.

There, off to one side, in the bottom of a crater about the size of a football field, stood a half-circle of white columns, in the fluted Doric style—Catie had done more than enough columns in her *Appian Way* piece, and knew Doric from Ionian when she saw it. Some of the columns were broken at their tops, and their capitals had fallen here and there. Other columns which should have completed the circle lay higgledy-piggledy on the ground like felled trees, shattered in their fall. In the middle of the circle, where the fluted remains of several columns lay across one another and left a little space, Mark Gridley was sitting on one column, as if on a bench, and leaning back against another. In the empty space before him a display window hung, and he was watching a football game.

Catie strolled over to him, raising dust, and stood by him for a moment, looking at the image. "Is this preseason," she said, "or post?"

Mark snorted. "Who can tell anymore?" He looked over his shoulder at her. "Sorry I've been hard to find lately."

"Don't sweat it, Squirt, I've been busy, too."

"So I hear." He waved at the viewing window, and it went blank. "James Winters said you needed to talk to me about some things."

"Yeah." She sat down on another of the columns, making herself as comfortable as she could on the ridges. "At the moment, I need to know just what makes a 'sealed' server sealed."

He grinned at her, an entirely happy look. "Want to break into one and find out firsthand?"

Catie had to sigh. "Mark, has anyone ever investigated whether you might possibly have some piracy in your background somewhere?"

"Might be, on the Thai side," Mark said cheerfully. "There were some funny things going on in the Malay Straits late last century. . . ."

"Don't tell me. I don't want to know."

"And my mom told me once that she was related to Grainne O'Malley. . . ."

Who? But Catie refused to ask him if this relationship was a good thing. Once you got Mark started on some subjects, there was no stopping him.

"I'd prefer not to break in anywhere we're not wanted," Catie said. "Life is complicated enough at the moment. But I also need to talk to you about some structural issues."

"That's what Winters said," said Mark. "So, shoot."

"Well, first, the spatball servers. 'Sealed' how, exactly?"

"Triple-redundancy controls on access to the code," Mark said. "And safe-deposit type security on the physical servers themselves—three-key access, with the highest officials in the organization holding the keys. It's sort of like the way they used to handle missile launches last century. However," Mark said, and smiled a completely unnerving smile, "any security that human beings devise, human beings can defeat. With time, and care, and enough brains."

"Fishing for compliments, Mark?"

He didn't deign to answer that. "As regards the ISF servers, though," Mark said, "I can save you some time and worry. Net Force has already been through those with a fine-tooth comb."

"Meaning you, I take it."

"I went along for the ride," Mark said. "Nothing showed up."

"Did the software people who normally maintain the code know that you were coming?"

"No. Well, yes," Mark said after a moment. "Upper management knew, since we were doing a physical-equipment assessment as well. In fact, the ISF asked us to come in as soon as Net Force contacted them."

"Then we can assume that 'lower' management knew about the inspection, too," Catie said. "Wouldn't you say?"

"Seems likely enough. Assuming 'worst case,' anyway."

"I think you may as well assume it. I suspect your dad would have, anyway." Catie thought for a moment. "Okay . . . so they'll have had time to hide things from you, if anybody on the 'inside' wanted to. . . . Even though you've already been in there, I'd like a quick look around in that server. Can you finesse it?"

Mark looked at her for a few moments, a very speculative expression. "Catie, I'm not sure this is strictly the kind of help James Winters had in mind when he brought you on board."

Catie swallowed. "I can't help that," she said. "There are things I need to look at before I can figure out what questions to ask George Brickner. It's no use wasting his time and mine running down one blind alley after another. And anyway, if I don't understand the inside of the server technology well enough to know what to listen for, I'm going to be wasting my own time, too . . . not to mention that I won't be able to help your friends at Net Force in what they're trying to achieve."

Mark thought about that for a moment. Then his face cleared. "All right," he said. "I know you can be trusted. And there's no time like the present. Come on!"

He jumped up and led Catie off to one side, away from the fallen pillars. "Yo, cousin," Mark said to his work-space management program.

"Working."

"Access doorway. Crapshoot."

"Opening access now, and logging." A blue outline appeared in the empty "vacuum" before them, and filled itself with darkness.

"Logging to my storage only," Mark said hastily.

"Logging limited," his workspace management program said, and the blackness in the doorway shimmered. A different quality of darkness, with a vague bloom of light in the background, was all that Catie could see through it at the moment.

"That's so my dad won't find out about this immediately," Mark said. "But, Catie, he's going to have to know sooner or later. So don't do anything that's going to make Net Force look stupid later on."

"As if I would," Catie said.

"I know. But I have to say it anyway." The look he gave her was surprisingly fierce, and it amused Catie a little to find that he was so territorial . . . and pleased her as well. She knew some of the older Net Force Explorers who were friends with him had an idea that Mark might be slightly uncontrollable, even unprincipled, but plainly there were things that mattered to him . . . and for Catie, this was a source of some relief.

They stepped through together. Inside the doorway was

a wide dark plane, all ruled with green parallel lines crossing one another and stretching to infinity in all directions: a naked Cartesian grid, unfeatured, like a space that hadn't even been configured yet, and with only two dimensions detailed.

"This is kind of minimalist, isn't it?" Catie said, looking around.

Mark nodded. "The ISF's senior programmers seem to like it that way. No obvious cues."

"I'll say," Catie said.

"However," Mark said, "*I* am not one of their senior programmers. I prefer my programming a little more objectified. And between you and me, so do their more junior programmers . . . as you'll see."

He reached into the darkness, and then in one gesture flipped a panel of the empty air up as if it were a little door. Under the panel, hidden in the same way that a car's gas cap might be hidden under the fueling flap, was a square of light, and in the square, Catie saw a big obvious keyhole.

"No use in having a back-door key," he said, "if you can't use it occasionally." He reached into his pocket and pulled out an unusually large key, apparently made of some metal that was green in the same way gold was gold-colored. Mark pushed the key into the keyhole, and turned.

The whole Cartesian "landscape" shimmered, wavered . . . and vanished. For a moment the two of them stood alone in total darkness. Then slowly starlight began to fade in around them, and from off to one side, a great bloom of cool blue light became apparent.

Catie looked that way and took a deep, sharp breath. Under them, in darkness, the Earth was turning. They were standing in emptiness about five thousand miles out, on the "dark side" at the moment. The spatters of light that were the great cities of the North American continent were glowing beneath them. In the Pacific they could see another faint glow of light, silvery and diffuse, and Catie looked over her shoulder to see the full moon looking down at its own reflection, setting, as away over at the other side of the world, another light grew.

Slowly the sun began to climb in growing glory through the atmosphere, the light of it burning red at first as it shone through the air's greatest thickness, then burning paler, orange, golden, white, and then utterly blinding as it came up over the terminator, and the fire and light of day swept across the Atlantic toward New York.

"Catie?"

"Yeah?" she said, not much wanting to be distracted from this gorgeous view. Whether it was based on real-time imaging or was someone's reconstruction, it was beautiful.

"Catie!"

"Yeah, *what?*"

"Duck!"

She looked at Mark and wondered what his problem was ... then, at the very edge of her peripheral vision, caught something, another bloom of light from behind them, the wrong direction. Something was falling at her, fast. Out of reflex, she ducked, turning—

Blazing in the new sun, silent as a feather falling through air, it came plunging at them seemingly right above their heads, immense, unstoppable, massive, but still graceful in its motion: a space station, a nonexistent one—for no one had ever actually built a space station along the "traditional" lines that were first mooted in the middle of the last century, a wagon wheel with spars outreaching from a central hub. The silvery-white-skinned bulk of it passed so close over their heads that it seemed impossible to Catie that it wouldn't stir up wind and ruffle their hair. But they were in "vacuum," and there was no wind, and no sound, just the vast mass of the station passing over, passing by, gone—silhouetted now against the steady, unbearable fire of the sun, and receding from them as it plunged on past at thousands of miles per hour, rotating gracefully around its hub as it went.

"Nice, huh?" Mark said, getting up and dusting himself off.

"Yeah, nice," Catie said, getting up, too. "You might have warned me a little sooner."

"What, and spoil the effect? Someone here went to a lot of trouble to write that routine. It's the server-maintenance people's intro to the space . . . I thought you might like to see it."

There was no question that it had been worth seeing, but Catie wasn't going to admit that to Mark right this minute. She looked after the space station as it receded, noting the structure of the hub. Rather than having a docking facility there, it was just a blind sphere. "Is that spat volume?" she said.

"Yup," Mark said. "It's the external 'restatement' of the shell that holds the rules for the behavior of the internal volume. The volume's been instructed to act like the 'classic venue,' the original Selective Spin module that they hooked up to the International Space Station. But the designers prefer this for the outside. It's prettier, and doesn't look like it was built by a committee."

There was no arguing that. "How do we get in?" Catie said.

Once more Mark reached into his tame "flap" of empty space and fiddled with a control. Some hundreds of miles from them, the space station froze in place, and the sun stopped rising, then the space station seemed to rush toward them again, at an even higher speed than it had originally swept by. Catie felt like ducking again, but she stood her ground. The station plunged right at them, and then swept through them in a blur of cutaway views too swift to grasp. A moment later she and Mark were standing in the middle of the spat volume at the heart of the station, not even its goal hexes showing at the moment, only a dim silvery light illuminating the cubic while it was in standby mode. The space was anechoic, empty, and just on the borderline of cold.

"This is 'where' it happens," Mark said. "The visual aspect of it, anyway."

"Maybe we should look at the nonvisual aspect," she said.

"The code? Sure. It's mostly written in Caldera, except for the imaging calls."

"Oh, joy," Catie said. She had been working for some time to learn Caldera, one of the main languages that simulation builders and the designers of virtual environments used, because she had to. It was the "framework" on which imagery was hung. But the language was not proving easy for her to master. To get your imagery to move and act as if it were real, the image you constructed had to exchange its motion "calls," the instructions you built into it, with the program underneath. The two sets of programming had to work flexibly together—but at the moment Catie knew the imaging program, the "muscles" and "skin" of any given environment, a lot better than she knew the underlying structural code, the "bones." In her earliest virtual work, this had been a matter of preference, and she had worked as she pleased, with what languages and utilities she pleased, ignoring the "hard parts." However, now that she was beginning to approach professional levels of work, she could no longer allow herself the luxury of such preferences, at the risk of marginalizing herself and limiting the kinds of artwork she could do. Catie was having to come to terms with those underlying "bones," and with the concept that an environment sometimes had to be built from the inside out. She was beginning to work out how to handle this new way of constructing images and simulations—she had no choice—but she knew that for a good while now it was going to make her brain hurt. Catie eagerly awaited the "paradigm shift" when it would all, suddenly, make sense, and the two ways of constructing virtual imagery would unite and knit themselves into a seamless whole . . . but she had no hope of having this happen to her in time to do her any good in this particular situation. *I'm just going to have to muddle through the best I can. . . .*

"Okay," Mark said, "here's the Caldera structure." And he turned the key again.

The image of the spat volume disappeared. It was replaced by a towering construct of lines and curves and helices and geometrical solids of light, reaching up and up and up into darkness. Every one of those objects or lines meant a line of code, or a set of instructions based somewhere outside of the program itself, "Oh, no," Catie said, and covered her eyes for a moment, just sheerly overwhelmed. *I hate abstract code presented this way, I hate it! And just* look *at all this!* There had to be hundreds of thousands of lines of code here. . . .

"Sorry, Catie," Mark said, but he sounded a little bemused by her distress. "It's the naked code, yeah, but it's simpler to look at it this way than if you objectify it. That just complicates matters. If you want, I can try to find you another paradigm. . . ."

"No," Catie said, "maybe it's better if I just try to make sense of it this way." She stared up at the construct, craning her neck. It seemed to be about the height of the Eiffel Tower. After a moment she said, "Is there a legend?"

"Sure," Mark said, and fiddled with his invisible "controls" again. A "legend" window popped out to one side of where they stood, showing examples of the graphical structures used to indicate the program's code, and next to each one a text description of the kind of code involved—structural, procedural, object-specific, referential, and so on. Catie stared at it with some dismay. It was going to take her days to come to grips with this.

"Is there a way to highlight the strictly image-related lines and linkages?" she said. Better to start with the parts she would be immediately familiar with, Catie thought, and then work inward to the less familiar ones.

"Sure," Mark said. He reached over to the legend window and touched the taskbar down at the bottom. It immediately displayed a master menu with a gridfull of glowing icons, one of which looked like a small picture in a frame. The construct in front of Catie changed, about 80 percent of the curves, lines, and squiggles fading away to shadows of themselves, and leaving a great number of solids of various shapes shining in various colors.

"There you are," he said. "The ones in a single color are single images or stills; striped or shaded ones are composites or motion clips. You can have the construct slide itself down through the 'plane' we're standing on, or move the plane up and down, to get at a given image. Take it out of the construct and it'll expand itself in the space and show you the image or 3-D construct. When you do that, an editing window drops down at the same time. But I wouldn't edit anything if I were you."

"Before I knew what I was doing," Catie said, "definitely not. And probably not even then." She looked up at the massive structure. "James Winters suggested to me that you'd been working with this for some while...."

Mark nodded. "It's complex, but not beyond managing," he said. "Mostly I've been working with the senior Net Force program analysts to look for signs of tampering—we've been comparing the code against the initial archival copies of the server program, and the more recent backups, to see where there've been changes."

"And you haven't found anything to suggest what's going on?"

Mark shook his head, and scowled.

"Did you look at the image calls?"

"We gave them a once-over, yeah, to see if whoever was tampering might have tried to make it 'look like' one thing was happening, say a near-miss on a goal, when something else should actually have happened instead. But we didn't find anything of that sort."

So much for my first bright idea. And my main area of expertise . . . and any hopes of figuring this out in a hurry. Catie was suddenly filled with dismay. She had given James Winters her best "I know what I'm talking about" performance, and it was all going to come to nothing. She was going to look like a complete fool. . . . *Well, maybe I will . . . but I'm gonna do my darndest to be useful anyway. For George's sake, if nothing else.*

"Tell me something," Catie said. "Are *you* strictly supposed to be in here at the moment?"

"Wellllll . . ."

"Never mind," Catie said. "I should have known."

"But I just can't let it be," Mark said. "You know how it is, Catie! You start working on something that matters . . . and you can't let it be." He gazed up at that towering structure with an expression that suggested the same kind of frustration that Catie felt from just looking at it. "I've been all over it with the experts, and I can't figure out what's wrong. We know somebody's messing with the server's programming somehow . . . we're *sure* they are. But we can't find out how. If *you* can turn up anything, anything at all, no matter how small or odd it seems to you . . ."

Catie sighed. "Mark, I'll do my best. But I'm going to need a fair amount of time with this."

"Lucky for you the server's down, except for testing, until Thursday," Mark said. Ceremoniously he presented her with the shining green key that symbolized the access routine. "I'll give you a copy of the testing schedules, so you can avoid those times, if you want to. Otherwise, don't do anything I wouldn't do."

Catie privately thought that this injunction left her entirely too much room to maneuver. "You said that access to the space is usually a triple-key business," she said. "I take it that this little gadget"—she hefted the key—"gets around that."

"It does," Mark said. "It also makes the bearer operationally invisible. Even if the invigilators came into the server while you were working, and you had that with you, they shouldn't be able to tell a thing." He looked rather pleased.

"And your dad knows about this?"

"Um—as I said—"

"Right," Catie said, and sighed. "I'll keep my incursions to an absolute minimum, and I won't meddle with anything I do find. But if as you say no one's going to be running a game on the server until Thursday, I should have at least a little time. . . ."

"Let me know if you find anything at all," Mark said. "Here, lend me that for a moment."

She handed him the key. Mark pushed it once more into his little flap in space. A moment later they were standing once more on the moon, with the crescent Earth back in the sky again, among the fallen columns.

Mark handed Catie back the key, and she slipped it into

her kilt pocket, glancing around her. "I have just one question for you," she said.

"Yeah?"

She waved one hand at the columns. "What're all these about?"

"Uh . . ." Mark looked suddenly shy, an expression that sat very oddly on him. "I'm rebuilding it."

Catie blinked, for she had begun to recognize the worn and pitted look of these columns. "You're going to rebuild the temple of Apollo at Corinth?"

"Uh, yeah," Mark said. "It's to go with that."

He pointed. Catie looked in the direction Mark was indicating . . . and saw, off in the distance, a twin of the Vehicle Assembly Building at Cape Canaveral, towering up against the hard, jagged black horizon like a giant child's block dropped there and forgotten.

Catie had to smile.

"Right," she said, and declined to tease him . . . for the moment. It was always adorable to find that someone you thought of as utterly practical was in fact a romantic, in love with that first great venture off the planet. "Mark, are you going to be working at this for a while more?"

"Yeah," he said. "The key you have is a copy."

"Okay," she said. "I may be in touch later."

"Right." As she turned away, Mark added, "Good hunting."

I sure hope so, she thought, and stepped through the doorway back into her space.

Catie took only a moment to glance at the chessboard to see if there had been any change there, or whether there was a text window with a new move waiting for her. There was neither, but she heard a soft sound from not far away inside her space, and turned to see what it was.

Her mother was standing at the back of the Great Hall, on the reading room side, looking at something in a glass case. Catie wandered over there to look over her mother's shoulder. The case contained one of the library's great treasures, a Gutenberg Bible; each day it was turned to a different page, not just to show off the engravings, but because (as her mother had told her often enough) a book's purpose is to be opened, and looked at, not kept locked in a vault somewhere . . . and the rarer the book, the more this was true.

"You home from work, Mom?"

Her mother was leaning in close to the glass to examine an elaborate letter *M*, printed in a block of red up against the left-hand margin of the left-hand page. "Half an hour or so ago," she said. "Your dad bent my ear briefly about your friend George. And Net Force."

"Uh-huh," Catie said.

Her mother turned away from the book. "You were telling him that James Winters said this wasn't going to be dangerous for you."

"That's what he said. He also said you should call him if you have any questions."

"I'll be doing that shortly." She looked across the Great Hall to where Catie's chair sat, with the simulacra of canvases and piles of paper all around it. "But not with questions, really. I trust you to have accurately described what's going on, and on the basis of that, your dad and I think you should go ahead."

"Uh, okay." Catie blinked. It hadn't occurred to her that matters were going to work out this simply.

"I mean," her mother said, "if we've managed to raise you so that you're concerned enough, on discovering crooked dealings, to want to do something about them, to stop them—then maybe we shouldn't be complaining too much about it. Much less trying to stop you, as long as what you're doing isn't going to endanger anyone. Especially yourself . . ." Her look was wry. "And besides, if things go the way you want them to go, after college, and you do wind up applying to enter Net Force—well, a little early involvement couldn't hurt, could it?"

"Actually," Catie said, "no. Thanks, Mom . . ." She slipped one arm around her and gave her a quick hug.

Her mother chuckled and hugged her back. "I know that tone of voice," she said. "I used to sound that way myself when I was your age and I would think, 'Wow, my mother's so much less dumb than she was when I was younger.' "

Catie burst out laughing.

"The only condition is that I want you to keep me posted with whatever's going on," her mom said. "Don't hesitate to call me at work if you need me."

"Do I ever?"

"No comment. But if there's trouble, I want to be the first to hear about it, unless your dad's in the house. No sitting on little fires until they're infernos before you call for help, understand?"

"Okay."

"Good. So get yourself out of here in an hour or so . . . dinner'll be ready then."

"What're you making?"

"Hey, it's not my night to cook," her mother said. "I have some reading to do. Your dad's making lasagna."

Catie's mouth immediately began to water. "Fifty-nine minutes, you said?"

"Why don't I get that kind of response for my beef stew?" her mother said. "Ingrate! I take back everything I said about how well we've brought you up." And, laughing, she vanished.

Catie spent about half that hour reviewing the copy of the Caldera online manual that she kept in her workspace. Some of the commands she knew well enough, since the imaging tools she used most often shared them. Some were completely unfamiliar, and now she kicked herself for having been so selective about her use of this particular resource . . . especially because there were aspects of Caldera so powerful that Catie started to get the feeling that she had been making herself work harder than she had to. Now she sat looking at lists of commands that she had very little time to master, and feeling dumber than usual.

When I go in there and start looking that program over, she thought, *what's to say that I won't look right at the answer and not recognize it because I was too lazy or too unnerved to study this stuff thoroughly—*

"Hello?" a male voice said.

Catie's head jerked away from the manual "pages" that were hanging in the air all around her. The voice had not been that of her father or brother. "George?"

"Can I come in?"

"Sure, if you don't mind a mess . . ."

George stepped in out of the empty air and looked around him with surprise, and then pleasure. "I would not call this a mess," he said. "You built this?"

"I mocked it up," Catie said.

"Nice job!"

"Uh, I was faking it," Catie said, feeling that this assessment was more than usually true, while George did what just about every visitor to either the real Great Hall or Catie's duplicate did—stood there craning his neck at the paintings and mosaics under the ceiling.

"If this is faking it," George said, "I'd like to see what your real work looks like."

"Um," Catie said, biting back about five possible self-critical remarks that she could easily have made. It was the one way she took after her father. Catie preferred to run herself down so that anyone else intending to do so would find that the job had already been done by a resident expert. "Thanks."

"I had a move," George said, "but I thought I might bring it over, if you were available, instead of just mailing it in."

"Sure, go for it."

George stepped over to the chessboard and picked up a bishop which he had moved out earlier. Now he advanced it a little further along a different diagonal.

"Space?" Catie said.

"I'm so glad we're on a first-name basis," said the voice out of the air.

George laughed.

Catie raised her eyebrows. "Log that, will you please?"

The text window hanging in the air promptly added a line:

Catie looked at the move, and also looked at the way George was regarding the chessboard: looking more or less at it, but now suddenly not seeing it, or much of anything else, from the concerned expression on his face.

"Can I offer you a chair?" Catie said.

"Uh, yeah."

She made him one, a "comfy" one like hers, but not so beat-up, and had her space put it over by the chessboard. George sat down and stretched himself, and sighed a little.

"Did you have a practice today?" Catie said.

"Huh? Oh, yeah," George said. "Some of the guys have been having their machines checked over by their service providers before the tournament, so we wanted to run them in and make sure everything was okay."

"I guess that's why you're looking like you're incredibly worried about something," Catie said.

George looked at her with astonishment. "I wasn't— was I—I mean, I—" Then he stopped, and smiled, a rather sad smile. "It shows that much, huh?"

"If you painted the words *scared and upset* on your forehead, it might just give me a clearer hint," Catie said, "but only just. George, what's the matter?"

He sighed.

"Pressure's piling up, huh . . . ?"

"Not just pressure." George leaned back and looked at Catie and let out another breath. "More than that. Something worse."

Catie sat and waited, and didn't say anything.

"Well, I mentioned to you that we had an invigilator call up, didn't I? That was Karen de Beer."

"Yes?" Catie said.

"Well, she was invigilating a non-ISF server game. You can't use the noncertified servers for tournament play, but a lot of teams have licensed the server software from the ISF for use in their informal or 'fantasy' play. Though the servers aren't used for formal tournament play, the ISF sanctions their use in 'fantasy' tournaments and informal regionals. Karen went off to invigilate at a game between Denver and Flagstaff, and . . ." He trailed off.

"And what?"

George was looking even more uncomfortable. "Catie . . . I really shouldn't be telling anyone this."

She opened her mouth to say "Then don't tell me," and then closed it. Catie got up, went over to the chessboard for a moment, picked up one of her knights, and moved it to threaten one of George's front-rank pawns.

For a long moment George sat there, saying nothing. Then he looked up at the dome of the Great Hall and said, "I trust you, Catie. And I don't know who else to tell. . . . Some guy came to the door of Karen's apartment this morning. He said he liked the way she'd handled the game at Denver . . . and he wanted to know, did she want to make some extra money."

"Doing what?" Catie said, sitting down again.

He looked at her with an expression that seemed to say, *Can't you guess?* "He said he represented some people who wanted Karen to invigilate spat games that they were going to be running out of another server, a private server that his people were going to be setting up. Now, this kind of thing happens . . . but never outside of the auspices of the ISF. The Federation publishes a list of non-tournament servers that have been inspected by them and passed for use by ISF member teams and team-candidates, spatball groups that are still serving their qualification period. Federation members don't do invigilation work outside of the 'passed' servers; at least, not if they want to stay in the Federation."

George got up and walked around the chessboard, looking at it. "It's tricky business, invigilating a spat space," he said, not looking at Catie. "Besides consulting with the referee before and during the game, you have to make sure that all the parameters for temperature and air density and rotation and friction and elastic collisions and so forth are set correctly in the software, and that they stay that way—that play, or hardware or code errors, which turn up sometimes, don't alter them, so that play stays fair. There are about fifty sets of parameters that have to be managed during the course of a match, and you have to watch them all, all the time, and be ready to alter them if the computer messes them up. It's real easy to handle a space incorrectly, get things wrong, if you don't have enough experience. More . . . if you *are* experienced . . . it would be easy enough to set the parameters wrong on purpose. Or to let other people see how it could be done."

"And Karen thought they wanted her to do something like that."

"That, or something similar." George breathed out, went around to his king's knight and picked it up, walked out onto the board and set it down. The notation window flickered and said K-KB3. "The guy named a figure . . . said Karen could start any time."

"What did she say?"

"She said she'd think about it. She told me yesterday that she was still thinking about it. She works in a convenience store, Catie. The figure was about three times her year's salary. And she's by herself, don't forget, and she has a little girl to support."

"I don't suppose he left her a Net address," Catie said.

"He said he'd come back in a few days and see what she had to say." George looked at his move as if he was most dissatisfied with it. "He told her not to mention it to anyone, or there could be trouble. She told me . . . and now she's scared. But she would have been scared even if she hadn't told me, she said. And she's scared for her little girl, too, for Carmen. Karen's not stupid. She knows trouble when she sees it. She temporized . . . out of shock, I think. She was never in any doubt that she wanted nothing to do with the offer. But now she's afraid of what the guy might say if she tells him no."

Catie swallowed. This was something that James Winters was definitely going to need to hear about. *As long as no one notices them contacting her* . . . But naturally Net Force would have ways to do that discreetly.

She swallowed again. "I don't suppose that anyone else on the team's had anyone approach them that way," Catie said.

George shook his head. "If they have, I haven't heard about it. Got another move?" he said.

"I'm thinking about it." But strategizing her next move

was actually buried behind four or five other, more immediate concerns at the moment.

When she looked up, she found George looking at her
again. It was another of those distressed expressions,
though this time he was at least trying to hide it. To Catie,
the effect was simply as if he now had NOT REALLY UPSET
painted on his forehead . . . and suddenly she knew what
the problem was, or thought she did.

"Look, I—"

"George," Catie said, sounding extremely severe and
for the moment not caring, *"it's not like that.* You think
you have a monopoly on 'not married, not dating, not gay,
and no plans'?"

He just kept looking at her. Then he sagged. "Uh," he
said, "maybe I'm doing you an injustice. It's just that it's
rare . . . and seems to be getting rarer . . . to find friendship, in my situation. Just plain friendship. Sorry."

"Well," Catie said, and let it sink in for a moment. "All
right. What are you going to do?"

"I don't know," he said. "Tomorrow morning is the
draw. The play-offs will start on Thursday at the soonest,
maybe Friday. Karen's going to have to do something.
I've got to find a way to protect my team. . . ."

"If there's anything I can do to help," Catie said after
a moment, "let me know."

George got up slowly, looking down at the chessboard
again.

"Call me when you have a move," he said. "I'll talk to
you later."

And he went through the door that had been standing
waiting for him off to one side, in the air, and it closed
behind him.

Catie sat very still for some while, considering possible
moves in two very different games.

6

She took the predictable amount of teasing about being late for dinner, and Hal punished her for this slight on her father's cooking by the most straightforward means possible—eating most of the lasagna and leaving Catie just enough for one serving, and nothing at all for seconds.

When she complained, her father threw his hands up. "It's all I could do to get him to leave the pattern on the plates," he said. "At least there's some sauce left. Make some pasta."

Normally a turn of events like this would have left Catie furious. Tonight, though, she simply made pasta, completely confusing Hal, who had been expecting—looking forward to, in fact—a far more explosive response. When Catie finished gobbling up her pasta and went straight back into the family room to use the Net machine, she heard Hal saying under his breath to her father, "You think she's coming down with something?"

She ignored him, got straight back into her workspace, and got back to work reviewing Caldera. Several hours passed, at the end of which her brain was buzzing with commands and obscure syntaxes that she had never thought she'd need any time soon.

But I need them now, she thought, getting up out of the Comfy Chair at last and picking up, from the floor beside the chair where she had left it, Mark's shining green key.

She pulled down a window to check the schedule he had sent her of the maintenance schedule for the ISF server. Theoretically no one would be in there until tomorrow morning sometime—local time, anyway. That was the afternoon for her, since the server itself, and most of the techs who managed it, were on the West Coast. All the same, Catie was twitching as she held the key up. "Space?" she said.

"You're gonna get in *trou*-bllle . . . *you're* gonna get in *trou*-blle. . . ." her workspace manager sang, sounding entirely too gleeful about it.

"Not nearly as much as Mark Gridley's gonna be in when all this is over," Catie said grimly. "He's gonna wish the Sureté had kept him to play with. Listen, you, just open a door to get me into the ISF server. The specs for the gateway are all right here. Don't deviate, or I'll pull your wires out, tie them to the tree in the front yard, and chase you around it."

"Uh," said her workspace manager. An open gateway popped into existence in front of Catie. Through it she could see darkness, with green lines drawn through it, running away to eternity. . . .

"Keep this open in case I need to leave in a hurry," Catie said.

"I, for one, intend to disavow any knowledge of your actions," said her workspace manager helpfully.

"You do that," Catie said, and stepped through the doorway into the dark of the spat-volume server's space.

She spent her first few minutes there just standing, looking around her, listening, for any sense or sign that anyone else might be here. But Catie heard nothing, saw nothing, but the Cartesian grid running off in its single plane into the empty darkness. Finally she lifted the key and pushed it into the darkness.

Obediently it cracked open before her to show her the keyhole. She turned it, and found herself, not standing in space this time, but floating inside the spat volume at the heart of the "space station."

"Workspace manager . . ." Catie said.

"Listening, visitor."

"Please show me the schematic of the server software that I viewed when I was last here."

The image of the spat volume around her faded away, leaving her standing on the Descartean plane again. But this time the server's software structure towered up in front of her once more, a skyscraper's worth of code, all represented once more as squiggles and bright colors and straight lines and wavy lines and spheres, like a spaghetti-and-meatball dinner with aspirations to architecture. Catie heaved a big sigh. "All right," she said to herself, "time to start trying to figure this thing out. . . ."

She sat down on the green-lined "floor" and considered where to begin.

Elsewhere, hidden away in the depths of virtuality in a dim blue-lit bar that might or might not have genuinely existed somewhere else, two men more thoroughly wrapped in shadows than ever sat on either side of one of the marble tables and studied it and their drinks, trying to avoid having to look at one another. Even here, wearing seemings, neither of them raised his voice above a whisper . . . though the anger in their whispers plainly indicated that both of them would have liked to shout.

". . . They shouldn't have scored at all! Next time—"

"Forget next time for the moment! We're not done with last time. And they *did* score." Darjan was glaring at Heming. "What do I have to do to get through to you how important this is? You need to have these routines correctly implemented by Thursday, and the people handling them clued in about what needs to be done, or there's going to be more than just your ass on the line, my friend." The words were spoken in a way that had nothing friendly about it at all.

"So we'll have them ratchet the response up a level or two."

"Better make sure it's ratcheted up enough. . . ."

"Too much," said Heming hotly, "and it's going to start being obvious to the players. Then where will you be? You'll have an independent investigation breathing down your back before you know what's happened. Or worse still, Net Force will get involved. And then you, *my friend*, will find out what having your ass on the line really looks like." He watched Darjan for his response.

Darjan just stretched his legs out and turned his glass around on the table a couple more times. "Get it handled," he said. "There are enough bucks being bet on Chicago at the moment that it has to be right. The gentlemen upstairs want plenty of point spread on this result."

"Look, I told you, it's being handled right now. Correction has already been put in, and the techs are training on the 'twinned' server right now. They've even suckered some spatball players into helping them test the volume."

"Are you crazy? If the ISF—"

"One of the people who's been around to reassure them *is* ISF . . . or so they've been told. Our corporate connection."

Darjan still looked uneasy. "If word of that gets out—"

"It won't. Our connection has impressed on all his minor-league 'helpers' how important it is to keep the news about the new server quiet, so as not to spoil the big publicity push when 'the people funding it' make the announcement. But the testing has been going on for a couple of days now, and the players haven't noticed a thing. You can practically pull the ball out of their hands and they assume it was their fault somehow."

Darjan mulled that over. "All right. I wouldn't mind seeing one of these test sessions."

"I can set that up for you any time. They're testing this afternoon, in fact. You can be an invisible watcher."

"All right." He took a drink of his virtual martini. "There hasn't been anyone messing around with the genuine ISF server, has there?"

"No need. Their own people don't have any reason to be there now. Their own routine checks have all passed off without incident. And there's no reason we would put our own operatives in there, or anywhere near it, so close to the play-offs starting. There's no need for it anyway. The 'remote controls' from our mirror server are all installed and ready to go."

"Then why didn't they work last time?" Darjan said. "Dammit, that should have been another clean win for Chicago. Is that damn team that inept?"

Heming frowned. "They can't all know about the 'adjustment,'" Heming said. "Unfortunately, a lot of them are honest. The team captain's dropped some broad hints in the right ears, but that's all he can do without having their own coach on his case. What do you want him to do, take out an ad on CNNSI saying *This is how the volume has been fixed so we can win?* All he can do is direct play toward situations that our monitor can use to best advantage. After that, it's still up to the team."

Darjan breathed out, annoyed. "I suppose," he said. "Well, I've made a visit or so myself in the past few days to see what can be done about the 'honesty' issue from inside several of the teams. We'll see how those pay off."

"And don't forget about those 'maintenance' visits I told you about," Heming said. "The installation of the conditional switching in the South Florida players' Net machines. We've got three in already. Some of these guys are fairly anxious to make sure their machines are serviced before the play-offs . . . they've been making it easy for us, and we should be able to get the whole team seen to before they play anybody. The eavesdropping buffers we're installing will telegraph the players' physical movements to our monitor handling the mirror server a half a second or so before they go to the real one, and give our own handling routines a chance to react to their plays before they even actually happen in the spot volume. Think of it as insurance. Whatever happens, it's a technology we can use elsewhere after these play-offs, in all kinds of sports."

Darjan still didn't look entirely reassured. "Well . . . it had better just go right this time, Heming. Otherwise your people and my people are the ones that will take the heat . . . and you and I are inevitably going to get singed. If not burnt to a crisp."

Heming shook his head. "Look, I understand your concern, but it's handled. Come by this afternoon for the 'training session' and see."

Darjan nodded, still frowning, and had another drink. Around the two of them, the shadows folded in close.

Two hours later Catie was still staring at the server software construct, from about halfway up its height—she had moved the "floor" up to look more closely at the way the solids symbolizing the images of the spat volume were hooked into the Caldera command substructure—and wondering, from the pain in her head, whether she was coming down with a migraine. *Probably not,* she thought. *Mom said Gramma always said she felt sick before one. And I don't feel sick . . . just stupid.*

She rubbed her eyes and stood up for the first time in an hour or so. *I guess I have to admit that Mark's right. It's not the imagery that's at fault. I've looked at all the "canned" images in the routine, and all the code for the imagery that's created "on the fly." Nothing's wrong with the code. The problem has to be somewhere else.*

There's nothing else I can do but start looking at all the rest of this to see if I can turn anything up.

But if the Net Force people haven't seen anything . . . what in the world makes me think that I'm going to? Just more overconfidence. She blushed at the thought of what she was going to say to James Winters when they debriefed at the end of all this. *"Sorry, I bit off more than I could chew, I don't have a clue what's going wrong." . . . So much for my chances of ever actually getting a job working for this man, or his organization. . . .*

Catie stood there with her arms folded for a while, realizing that she might be looking at the beginning of the death of a dream. *And what else do I do with my life if Net Force doesn't want me?* Catie thought, despondent. The time after high school, which had looked like a whole spectrum of new beginnings, now started to look like a dead end. *I guess I can find some kind of entry-level job in advertising art, something simple, or—*

Then Catie shook her head, feeling angry and helpless

for the moment, but not quite beaten yet. The future would take care of itself, but right now there were other things to think about. *For one thing, I'm getting moody . . . it's blood sugar, probably. I need a break.*

"Workspace management," Catie said.

"Listening, visitor."

"Hold this imagery in nonreadable memory for me, locked to my voiceprint. When I return, reset it."

"Done." The structure vanished.

Catie pushed the key into the darkness, and the gateway into her own space opened up again. She stepped through gratefully and waved it shut behind her. Immediately she felt a little more relaxed. All the while she'd been there she couldn't get rid of the idea that someone from the ISF was going to pop out of nowhere and demand to know what she was doing there. Or—in her more paranoid moments—she imagined that one of the shadowy people who'd been tampering with the space in the first place might come across her. She shivered at the thought.

Catie chucked the key onto the Comfy Chair, and yawned. She was going to have to turn in soon, but meantime there were still problems to handle before bedtime. She was going to have to get some kind of report together for James Winters, regarding what George had told her. There were a few odds and ends of schoolwork that she still needed to handle . . . nothing serious, fortunately. And as she looked over at the chessboard, she realized that she'd promised George another move, and for all she knew, he was sitting up waiting for it, glad to have something to distract him from the tensions surrounding the "lottery" draw in the morning . . . and other things.

She looked over the chessboard, taking a moment to more closely examine George's last move, and the state of the board in general. It was getting crowded toward the center of the chessboard as the beginning of the "midgame" settled in. A lot of pieces were set to attack a lot of other pieces . . . but neither of them had started the shin-kicking yet. It was as if George was waiting to see what Catie would do, whether she was going to become the "aggressor" in this game. *Though he's already getting pretty aggressive himself,* Catie thought, eyeing the way George had set his bishops up to control the diagonals. *Still . . . why wait to let him start the carnage? I'm sure in a mood to start a little myself at the moment.*

George was presently using one of his knights to threaten a couple of Catie's pawns in a "knight fork," but one of her own pawns was advanced far enough to be a threat to the knight in turn. Her attention until now had been on developing other pieces of her own. Now she let out a long annoyed breath, thinking *Why not?* She moved the pawn over one square diagonally, taking George's knight, and picked it up and carried it off the board to set it down on one side. "Space?"

"The final f—"

"Don't say it," Catie said, grim. "Just *don't* . . . I'm not in the mood. Send him that move, and make it snappy."

"Uh, yes, ma'am, right away, ma'am."

Catie sat down in the Comfy Chair again and contemplated the chessboard . . . but she wasn't really seeing it, for having made her move, her mind had now immediately reverted to the earlier problem. *All that code. But I have to find a way to look at it and see if I can turn something up. I can't get rid of the idea that the imaging calls are being manipulated in some way that we're not anticipating.*

And what human minds can devise . . .

Yawning, she got up again, went offline, and got up out of the implant chair to go make herself some more pasta.

Catie was up at about six the next morning. Her father was asleep, but she actually caught her mother in the kitchen, making one last cup of coffee before heading to work. "Got a project in the works, honey?" her mom said, stirring the coffee in her big British Museum mug as she made her way to the kitchen table, where the usual pile of books was waiting to be taken back to work.

"Yup," Catie said.

"The one I'm thinking of?"

"Yup," Catie said. She started making tea for herself, not unaware of her mother's eyes on her.

"Well," her mom said, "be careful." And she didn't say anything else, possibly perceiving that Catie wasn't worth much until she got some breakfast in her, and was going to be careful anyway. She finished her coffee in silence, taking just a few minutes to stand in front of the fridge and read the headlines from the *Washington Post* that were scrolling down the LivePad, then she picked up her books and her shoulderbag, kissed Catie, and headed out the door.

Catie was still sitting there about half an hour later, finishing her tea, now cold, and thinking about what George had said to her after "I shouldn't be telling you this." Not "Don't tell anyone else," not "I can trust you not to mention this to anyone," but simply "I trust you." Her conscience had been troubling her a little about the prospect of passing the information on, even though it had been freely volunteered. The feeling of discomfort had kept her from sending off the message to Winters last night, after she had gone online again and composed it. But once again Catie got the feeling that George was asking for help without actually saying so in the clear. *Maybe he's just being supercautious about the possibility he's being eavesdropped on. It's possible, I guess.*

She decided to set her concerns aside and send the message to Winters when she got back online. Meanwhile she had to get back to that horrible pile of code and finish looking over the imagery issues, no matter how she wished she could avoid it. She had slept badly, her dreams buzzing and writhing with lines of light that tripped and choked her, spheres and oblate spheres and ellipsoids and discs that dropped out of the tree of light onto her head and made it ache worse than ever. Yet at the same time she couldn't get rid of the idea that she might nonetheless be on the edge of finding out something useful.

Catie finished the cold tea, rinsed the cup out in the sink, went back into the family room, and got back online. In her space she saw that there had been another move in the chess notation window. BxN . . . *bishop takes knight,* she thought. *Yes, he's in the mood for shin-kicking too, now. Well, it'll have to wait a little while.*

Catie reached down to the floor beside her Comfy Chair and came up with the "key" again. "Space?" she said.

"You mean the authorities haven't come for you *yet*?"

Catie laughed. *I'm going to have to have a look at the management code myself,* she thought, *and see exactly how Mark programmed in all these rude responses.* "No," she said, "though the recycling people may be coming for *you* shortly. I'm sure you'll make somebody a terrific boat anchor. Meanwhile, just open my gateway to the server again."

The doorway appeared before her, outlined in light in the middle of the Great Hall. "Do you want your calls forwarded?" her space manager said.

"No, just flag me as unavailable unless it's my mom or dad or Mark."

Catie slipped through the doorway to stand once more on that wide, dark virtual plain, and paused there, letting her mind rest for a moment in the lines running to infinity in all directions, taking a moment to work out what she should do. She was still nervous, but as far as she could tell there was no one in here. This was another of the times that Mark had denoted as an "empty" period, and well out of hours for the server's staff, who after all out were on the West Coast somewhere. *A little early for them to be up,* Catie thought. *Then again, it's early for* me *to be up. So let's get on with this. . . .*

"Server management," she said. "Unlock the imagery from my previous visit."

"Voiceprint ID confirmed," said the server. "Representing structural model."

It appeared before her as it had the last time, that same massive structure of lines and curves and sections of geometric solids, all piled up in a single towering construct and here and there spilling over in what looked to her like disorganized heaps: a haystack in which the needle she was searching for might or might not be hidden.

"What a mess," Catie said softly.

Nothing's as complicated as it looks at first glance, she

heard her father saying, some time back, while they had been working on her geometry together. *Give it a moment, stand back, take it apart a piece at a time, and don't go to your fears for advice while you work. Use your brains. You've got plenty.*

And when brains run out, she heard her mother remark from somewhere nearby, *you can always fall back on stubborn. Sometimes it works nearly as well.*

Catie wasn't sure what there was left for her to "take apart" . . . at least, that she understood. Still, there were a couple of things she hadn't looked over in regard to the imagery—specifically the "insertions," the place where imaging instructions and calls interfaced with the actual structure of the server program. *If you were going to tamper . . . that would be a good place to do it.*

Not that the Net Force people wouldn't have thought of that, too. . . . Still, the stubborn was beginning to kick in, and Catie sighed and got on with it.

An hour or so later she was standing in the "air" about halfway up the structure of the program, and even in virtuality her eyes were beginning to get tired from tracing one connection after another, picking it up, looking to see how it interfaced with the next one along in the "chain." Each time she picked up one of the shining ropes that symbolized a command instruction, she had to pinch it in the place that would reveal its content, and then the actual text of the command would reveal itself in a text window nearby, and she would have to read it carefully, parsing it to see if it made sense in conjunction with the commands immediately preceding it or following it in the chain. The syntaxes were beginning to blur together, the terms had begun to reach that magic point where she didn't understand any of them anymore, the way you can stop understanding your own name if you say it three hundred times in a row.

Not too much more to do, thank heaven, Catie thought, vanishing one more text window and pausing to rub her eyes.

She picked up another command strand, a line of rose-colored light, and pinched it.

The lottery . . . It was some hours away yet, and she couldn't get her mind off it. The funny thing was that George hadn't seemed too concerned about which team South Florida actually wound up playing first. "In cold analysis, we're all pretty well matched," he'd said, "in terms of general strength. Sure, different teams have different specific strong areas. But we're so good as 'all rounders' that one team, really, is pretty much the same as another as far as I'm concerned." He'd smiled slightly when he'd said it. "We have one thing going for us that none of the others have. We all like each other. We're doing this for fun, because we enjoy playing together. None of the other teams can genuinely make that claim, since all their players are 'bought in,' one way or another."

"But will that matter at the championship level?" Catie had said.

"It'll sure matter if we lose," George had said, and laughed. "But we won't wind up hating each other. We *can't*. We shop for each other, we baby-sit each other's kids and help them with their homework, we go out for dinner together—did I tell you about the Dinner Brigade? A bunch of us are working our way through all the restaurants in the Miami Yellow Spaces. We're into the *D*'s now. A loss at this level will be real public, sure . . . but we're still going to be friends afterward. And spat is *a* basis for our friendships, but not *the* basis."

He'd leaned back and stretched again. "And on the other side of the equation," George had said, "the friendship might just help us win. We have a level of communication that the other teams don't always seem to have—or else theirs is an artificial thing, imposed, rather than something that grew naturally among the players. Is that enough of an edge? I don't know. The other teams have the advantage that they're professionals—they don't have to have day jobs, they can spend the kind of time practicing that we can only dream about. At the same time . . . *do* they spend that kind of time practicing? Maybe not. Like in parenting, there's a question of quality time versus quantity time. We may actually have an edge there. It's a job for them, not fun, the way it is for us. . . ."

Catie sighed, finished with that particular line of light, picked up another and read the command line in it, the name of the image file to which it attached, the programming instruction to which it interfaced at its far end.

I just hope he's right. It would be awful if the stress turned out to be too much for them, if their friendships or their personal lives started to come apart because of all the media attention. Like George saying that he couldn't even go to a convenience store without being followed. If I were in his position, I'd grab the first reporter I caught doing that and I'd—

Then Catie stopped, in complete shock, and stared at the thing she had been running idly through her hands. It was not a line of light after all. It was a text string. She had read it, she had understood it, she had finished with it, and had been about to put it back and pick up another, all without having to go through any laborious translation of the content—

And suddenly she realized what was happening. It was the paradigm shift, just a flicker of it. It had to be—though it wasn't even slightly as she'd imagined it would be if she ever achieved it. All this exposure to the raw code, which she hated—all the time Catie had been forcing herself to read it directly, something which she had always avoided—had started to force the change, and Catie was finally starting to think in Caldera. It was a revelation, like the day in her sophomore year when, without warning, after two years of classes and fairly uninvolving study simply designed to get her through her language courses with a passing grade, she had suddenly started to think in French. It was as if everything had been turned ninety degrees, somehow, and was being viewed from a different angle, one which had never been available to her before.

Wow, she thought. *I've got to get it back! How can I get it back? Everything was clear, there, just for a moment—*

Catie swept the key through the space in front of her, like a swordsman saluting an opponent, and reduced the huge structure before her to a gigantic tangle of bare code. Mark had been right. Objectifying the code just obscured the issue, concealing the instructions themselves. She needed to deal with them all at the component level.

Dad was right, she thought, *in a different paradigm. It is all just electrons. But if you understand the most basic building blocks of your medium, it doesn't matter whether you're working with "wet" ones or "dry" ones, or how many of them are strung together, or on what kind of framework—*

The code structure of the sealed server's operating programs stood before her now simply as text, hundreds and thousands and millions of lines of it. There was a temptation to panic at the sight of it all, but Catie restrained herself. The nature of programming being what it was, not all these instructions could possibly be unique. A lot of them would be copies of one another. Many of them would also be calling routines from outside the program itself, complex variables or constants that were defined in the Caldera language itself and lived on the master Caldera servers. Given the connectivity of the Net and the hundred-layer redundancy cushion that a "fundamental language" source like Caldera would maintain as part of its server infrastructure, there was no need for an end-user like the ISF ever to worry that Caldera's reference-variable resources would go down, and therefore there would be no need to waste space by keeping those variables and constants in ISF server space.

"Verbal input," she said to the ISF server manager.

"Accepted," said a woman's voice, dulcet and calm.

"Fade down all nonunique instructions," Catie said. "Highlight unique instructions, image calls, variable and constant calls to outside servers, and comments."

The structure shimmered like a cityscape with cloud sweeping over it, parts of it going vague, others burning bright in various colors. The unique instructions Catie ignored for the moment. She wanted first to look at the simple things again, the image calls and variables. There were fewer of them, and once she'd gone over them and gotten rid of them all, she could get on with examining the unique code and trying to understand it. *Which is going to take me until after the play-offs, probably . . .*

But for the moment Catie put that self-defeating thought away and made herself busy with the image calls nearest her. One by one she started checking the instructions again, referring them back to the images they called. The syntax was straightforward enough—a "connect" command, the identifier for the command to which it interfaced, a "call" command, the name of an image file, the size of the file, a specification for the size of its "display" as related to the frame of reference of the person experiencing it virtually, and a list of other files which would display "adjacent" to the file in question, changing as the one in this particular command line changed. Slowly, in flickers, unpredictably but in fits and starts that got more frequent the longer she did it, the "whole vision" of each command strand began to reassert itself. She was seeing them as single constructs, whole commands, not needing to spell them out laboriously, piece by piece. It was like the difference between reading one word at a time and taking a sentence as a whole. Catie started to speed up, pushing herself faster. *It's working. It's actually working—*

She finished going over the image calls in that region of the program in a fairly short time, and then stood there looking down from her height at all the rest of it, almost afraid to stop for fear that this new way of seeing the program might forsake her. *But what else is there really for me to do here? I should get out. At least, though, now I can pass this problem back to Mark with confirmation that the image calls are clear. No one is going to blame me if I can't make much of the rest of this. . . .*

Catie breathed out, feeling a kind of satisfaction even though she hadn't found anything really useful.

But, still . . .

Then, there alone in the darkness, she grinned. It wouldn't hurt to spend just a little more time, just to make sure the new perception wasn't a fluke.

"Down one," Catie said to the invisible pseudo-surface she was standing on. It obediently sank down a layer.

Catie grabbed another line of text, another image insertion call, she thought—then realized she had the wrong color of text: this one was a physical management command, one that handled the way people moved in this space. And a moment later, to her delight, she "got it" whole, without any real trouble—command, argument, force specifier, vector specifier, constant of mass, gravitational constant, constant of local light-speed in this medium, atmospheric density. Catie cracked the string of text like a whip, so that it burned briefly bright and dropped down all the additional notations and values for the constants, and she ran them through her fingers, pleased. She'd read this line as easily as the image calls, with all its dangling strings of digits and repeating decimals—

Catie paused for a moment, gazing down at one of the strands of digits hanging down from her hand from a glowing capital G, slightly larger than the other letters in that strand: the symbol for the gravitational constant. Below it the digits swung and dangled like a glowing chain: $6.6734539023956342\ldots\text{e-}11_1$, with the units signature "N m^2/kg^2" hanging there, like a charm, at the end.

. . . *Now what the heck's the matter with this?* For it didn't look right somehow. She had had occasion to use the gravitational constant once or twice when building the *Appian Way* scenario, because otherwise you couldn't walk through it correctly . . . and even the birds that flew through the scene wouldn't fly correctly until G was correctly in place. The fleeting thought of the former "George the Parrot" and his Gracie, and their chicks, made Catie smile a little at this connection, for she'd looked up the videos George had mentioned, and had seen the initial problems the birds had had in microgravity.

But Catie looked at that long decimal value of G now and couldn't understand the difference between the way it looked at the moment and the way it had appeared when she installed G into her simulation of ancient Rome, plugging it in via a live link from the "best current value" reference kept on the Public Ephemerides server that was jointly managed by the National Bureau of Standards and the Naval Observatory. She'd noticed a particular pattern to the fraction, a patch where the digits 3 and 9 repeated, . . . 393939, three times, and the peculiarity of the pattern had amused her. But now it went . . . 39023956. And there was an extra digit at the end of it. *What's that, an exponent or something?* But what would it be doing there? Anyway, the digit was below the main line of figures, not above it. *A footnote? Since when do constants have footnotes?*

"Where is this constant plugged in from?" Catie said.

"The constant is sourced locally," said the ISF server management program. "No remote link."

That's weird. Why go to the trouble to store it in this server when reference sources outside have the "freshest" version of the value? "What does that digit refer to?" Catie said, putting her finger on it, so that it glowed.

"Subsidiary instruction call," said the ISF server management program.

"I've never seen anything like that before," Catie said.

"Subscript digits are an optional command syntax expression in Caldera," said the server manager. "This is a 'legacy' expression common in earlier versions of the language and now routinely replaced in current command syntax by either the Boolean *or* expression or the '±' symbol and angle brackets enclosing the referent line or zone number."

Catie digested that for a moment. "Display the subsidiary instructions being called here," she said.

A text window opened off to one side, displaying about thirty command lines, one after the other. Catie started to read them.

They were all different versions of the gravitational constant. In some of them the numerical value varied just a little. In some, the variation was huge. What was even stranger was that many of them had an added string of data attached to them, vector specifications, as far as Catie could tell.

She shook her head, perplexed. *If I'm reading this right—these instructions, when they're called, would not only change the force of gravity in a space where they were brought into play, but change the direction in which it was pulling.* Even the biggest of the numbers were relatively small. Catie wasn't sure whether the changes would much affect something as massive as, say, a human being.

But a spatball—

Catie swallowed. George said it. *The ball didn't feel right. It didn't go where it was supposed to.*

And now she abruptly understood why. *Because someone, at the right time, was invoking these changed values for the gravitational constant.*

That's—that's—! The first word that occurred to Catie was *illegal,* though the word was faintly comical, used in this situation. Nonetheless, it was accurate; Catie was positively indignant at the sheer fraudulence of it. *You can't just change the laws of physics!* And Catie couldn't think of anything more basic to the way that objects in this particular frame of reference would operate.

And it'd be easy to miss. After all, who thinks about the gravitational constant? It's a constant!

. . . I've got to call Mark!

She checked her watch. It was eight in the morning. Any other time she would have thought "It's too early." *Now, though,* Catie thought, *If he's not up, it's about time he was!* But she wasn't comfortable about calling him from in here.

"Space," she said.

"Listening."

It's gotten so it feels weird not to be insulted, Catie said, and couldn't quite repress a smile despite the seriousness of the situation. "Save this configuration for me, voiceprinted again. Then close everything down."

"Done." The glowing tower of text vanished.

"Door," Catie said. Her gateway back to her space appeared before her. She slipped through it, waved it shut.

The first morning sun was glinting through the windows around the top of the reading room dome as Catie made her way back to the Great Hall. "Space!" she said.

"Now what?"

She grinned again. "Get me Mark Gridley, right now. Flag it urgent."

"Is he even going to be up yet? Growing boys need their rest." The tone of voice, if not the voice itself, was almost exactly Mark's.

"Get on it," Catie said, and picked up from the floor beside the Comfy Chair the piece of paper which stood for the virtmail she had been intending to send James Winters. "And see if James Winters is available, while you're at it."

There was a pause. A second later Mark appeared a few feet away.

"Oh, good," Catie said. "Listen, do you know what I found? There's—"

But Mark was speaking. "—not available right now, and I'm not sure when I will be. If you'll leave a message, I'll get back to you as soon as I'm free."

Oh, great! Catie thought. It was a recorded message again. It froze in place when it was done, leaving Mark standing there and looking slightly vague. *Now what? I can't tell James Winters about this! I wasn't even supposed to be in that space!*

But then Catie burst out in a sweat. If Net Force wasn't told about this right away, there was no telling what might happen during the play-offs. It wasn't just a matter of whether or not South Florida might win or lose. It was a matter of basic fairness, now, to all the other teams as well. . . . Not to mention not letting the bad guys get away with it!

And I have to talk to him anyway.

No point in putting it off.

Suddenly James Winters was standing there looking at her. "Uh, Mr. Winters," Catie said. "I have—"

"—apologies for leaving you a canned message. Unfortunately I'm away from my desk at the moment. If you'd kindly leave a message for me, I'll return the call as soon as possible. Thank you."

"Uh," Catie said. "Mr. Winters, it's Catie Murray. Please call me back as soon as you can. It's very urgent. Meanwhile I'm also sending you a report on a conversation I had with George Brickner. This is urgent, too . . . please get back to me soon. Thanks."

The image of Winters vanished. Catie glanced over and saw that the one of Mark had taken itself away as well.

"Wonderful," Catie muttered. There was nothing she could do now but go offline, go to school, and try to get hold of both Mark and Winters from there if she had time.

The two celebrities could have picked a specific ball on purpose. "First choice, please!" said the ISF president, who was acting as the master of ceremonies.

The woman and man each came up with a ball and

In a huge darkened space filled with the rustle and breathing of expectant people, one man in a dark AllOver suit stood at a "virtual podium," a reading window floating about chest height and tilted toward him. Off to one side, two other people stood by a table on which was a large cut-crystal bowl shaped like a spatball and containing a number of small opaque plastic balls.

"If our guests would go ahead and stir the choices—"

The two celebrity guests, a handsome tall dark man in a formal kilt and jacket with jabot and a blond woman wearing an electric-blue dress that covered her completely and yet left absolutely nothing to the imagination, both plunged a hand into the crystal bowl and started stirring. From somewhere a dramatic drumroll started to fill the space.

The stirring went on long enough and energetically enough to convince the most skeptical viewer that there was no way either of the celebrities in question could have picked a specific ball on purpose. "First choice, please!" said the ISF president, who was acting as the master of ceremonies.

The woman and man each came up with a ball and

handed it to the ISF president. This worthy, a short earnest-faced gentleman of Eastern extraction, proceeded to crack the balls open one at a time. From the first one a small spark of light burst out, floated up into the air, burning and growing, spinning and throwing off sparks like a Catherine wheel, and gradually turned into the famous red *M* and owl logo of one of the play-off teams.

"First to play in the quarterfinal series: Manchester United High—" A roar went up from the gathered Man United fans as the ISF president cracked open the second ball. Another spark of light shot out of it, leaped up into the air, and after a certain amount of shining and spinning, turned into a stylized flame surrounded by the letter *C*.

"—plays the Chicago Fire!"

Shrieks of delight from the Chicago contingent. The two logos charged at one another in the air, did a brief waltz around one another, and finally settled down to hang above and to the left of the ISF president.

"Second choice, please!"

The celebrities stirred the bowl again, each picked a ball, and once again handed them to the ISF official. He cracked the first of the two balls.

A streak of light arched up out of it and exploded into a miniature fireworks display overhead; after a few moments the fire faded away to show a stylized green grasshopper and the letters *XZS*. "In the second match, Xamax Zurich—"

The ISF president cracked the second ball open. The fireworks that went up were white at first, then turned yellow and black, leaving a yellow oval with two black spots at one end of it. "—plays South Florida Spatball Association!"

"Well, *good*," Darjan said, sitting back in his implant chair with a satisfied expression.

"Listen," Heming said to him, from nearby in the darkness of their joint experience of the lottery draw. "Didn't you hear what I *said*? *They've been in the server!*"

Darjan waved one hand in a languid way.

"What's the matter with you!" Heming said in an angry whisper. "If Net Force should find—"

"They nosed around for four days straight and didn't find *anything*," Darjan said, unconcerned, as he watched the draw for the third team to play begin. "We own somebody on the ISF's server maintenance team. He was looking over the Net Force geeks' shoulders the whole time. They went right through the system structure and couldn't find a thing wrong with it." And Darjan smiled.

"That they told *your* guy about, maybe!" Heming said. "What if they just want to catch our ops actually using the 'flipflop' instructions?"

"That's not going to happen," Darjan said. "The server issue is handled. Stop worrying about it, and just make sure those conditionals get used properly."

"And in the third match, the Rio de Janeiro Rotans—" said the ISF president.

"You saw the tests," Heming said.

"Tests are one thing," Darjan said. "Just make sure your people function at least that well on Thursday. What about those 'repairs' to the South Florida team's Net boxes?"

"—play the New York JumpJets—"

More shouting came from the selection ceremonies. "Which means that the Los Angeles Rams play Sydney Gold Stripe in the fourth match. And here's the play-off schedule—"

Heming scowled and waved the volume down. "Almost all done," he said. "The only ones not done now are the captains and two of the forwards. They'll be done today or tomorrow . . . plenty of time."

"Good." Darjan's smile persisted, and it wasn't particularly pleasant. "Not that they're likely to be a problem again in play. Xamax should wipe them up nicely even without help. But some of the principals want them out of the play-offs right away . . . they're still pissed off at the 'Kiwanis kids' having the nerve even to get into the same volume with Chicago last time, much less draw with them."

"Fine . . . we'll take care of it. What about your invigilator?"

"I have a call to her scheduled for this afternoon, just

before she goes to pick up her little honey from school. She'll play our side, I think."

Heming chuckled. "Well, then, we've got everything sorted out. This should be an interesting week. . . ."

Catie came home from school in a most unaccustomed rush. Normally she took her time on the combined ride and walk, letting herself depressurize after the day's work. Today, though, she came plunging in through the side door as if she were being pursued by wolves, and ran straight into Hal, nearly flattening him.

"Hey, look out, what's the matter with you?" he yelled at her. "Hey, not in there, I was going to go online, you can't—!"

Catie never heard what he said. She was in the implant chair, her implant lined up, within a matter of seconds. A few breaths later she was standing in the Great Hall. "Space—" she said.

"There you are," said her workspace manager. "I've been worried sick. There's a virtcall waiting for you. James Winters."

"Oh, thank heaven. Mr. Winters—"

He stepped straight through into her space. "Catie. Sorry I couldn't talk to you this morning. There were some things going on in the office." He glanced around. "Are we private at the moment?"

"Uh, yes."

"Do you have encryption?"

"Yes," Catie said, "I use DeepSatchel—"

"Would you turn it on?"

"Space?" Catie said.

"Listening."

"Go to encrypted mode and match to the remote encryption protocol."

"Done."

"Thanks," Winters said.

"And give Mr. Winters a chair!"

The same one he had used last time appeared. He seated himself. "Did your mother tell you she was going to speak to me, the other day?" Winters said.

"Uh, yes," Catie said. "It's been kind of busy—we haven't had a chance to touch base since then. We keep missing each other."

"The curse of modern life," Winters said. "We're more connected than we ever were, but no one seems able to keep in touch, even in the same house. Well, anyway, she'll have told you that she and your dad were happy enough for you to be working on this business, as long as due care was taken. Which obviously I promised her it would be."

He bent a rather thoughtful look on Catie. She instantly broke out in a sweat.

"Uh," she said. "Mr. Winters, I have a couple of things to tell you. But first of all, did you read what I sent you? It's really important."

"I read it," he said. "We're handling it. Some of our people are not too far from Karen de Beer's house right now. We'll be watching carefully to see if we can identify any visitor she has today . . . and whether they can be immediately identified or not, we're going to have a little talk with them after they leave. Nothing to do with the visit, of course. There are very few people on this planet who're perfect drivers, and some of our best operations on this continent start with the assistance of police officers who all of a sudden get very interested in someone's broken taillight, or the thickness of the tread on their tires." He smiled a very small smile. "Meanwhile, do you have anything else to tell me? My people and I have a busy evening ahead of us."

"Uh . . . Yes," Catie said, after what felt like one of the longest pauses of her life.

And then Catie told him about her access to the ISF server, and what she had found there.

During the fifteen or twenty minutes it took her to describe what had been going on, Catie watched Winters's face with increasing concern and could see nothing there at all. He might as well have been a carved statue, for all the reaction he showed. It was rather terrifying. Some change of expression might at least have given Catie a hint as to how to slant her story to her own best advantage while still telling him the truth. But Catie realized very quickly that Winters was not going to help her out that way, not by so much as a millimeter's worth of shift in the set of his face. So she told him the truth, as dryly as she could, with as little embellishment as she could manage; and then, when she ran out of truth, she just stopped.

Winters looked at Catie for a while without saying anything. It was probably only a few seconds. It felt like several years. And then he spoke.

"The *gravitational* constant," he said. His tone of voice, to her astonishment, was almost admiring, and not of her, as far as she could tell, but of the people who had sabotaged the ISF server. "Talk about hiding something in plain sight."

Catie, unable at the moment to do anything else, just nodded.

"So," Winters said. "Where do you think this takes us?"

Catie gulped, then got control of herself again. "Sir, George said the changes in the way the ball was behaving weren't constant. He said sometimes it seemed to act oddly, and sometimes it didn't. That, taken together with all those different 'definitions' of the constant, makes me think that there's someone, outside the server, using a remotely connected routine that acts as a kind of a switch. They watch the game, and throw the switch when it'll do the team they're backing the most good. Then they immediately put the constant back the way it should be again, so that no one will notice."

Winters nodded. "It does seem likely." He sat there brooding for a moment. "It would require some sophisticated programming calls to communicate with an outside source, probably some kind of mirror server, without triggering the ISF space's own alarms that its home server is being tampered with. But it could be done. Certainly it *can* be done, because it would seem it *has* been."

He looked at Catie then. "The one good thing about all of this," he said, "is that you've succeeded, through a combination of persistence and sheer dumb luck, in isolating a problem that our whole investigative team, and even Mark Gridley, couldn't find." Then the look turned chillier. "While also trespassing into a private server space, accessing copyrighted material without the copyright holder's permission, tampering with proprietary software, and possibly contaminating a crime scene."

Catie gulped again as the face she had been wishing would show some kind of expression, a few minutes ago, now showed one all too plainly.

"That said," Winters added, in a tone that was just slightly milder, "without what you've done, we wouldn't have any way to *prove* it was a crime scene. So that weighs down the scale a little in your favor. But I wouldn't get overexcited about that at the moment. Catie, this is *not* how we do business. This kind of stunt all too often results in criminals walking free when they would otherwise go for a long healthy sojourn in a residential facility with bars on the windows. Evidence *must* be acquired legally, right down the line . . . not just because that's how we get useful results in our business, but because it's *right* to do it that way. You follow me?"

Catie nodded, dumb.

"Now I have to work out how best to proceed here," Winters said, and looked down at his folded hands, and was quiet for a few moments.

Catie stood there and said not a word. The silence in the Great Hall became deafening.

"The audacity of it," Winters said then, "is just admirable. God knows how many virtual sports might have been subverted by this simple technique. But these guys have rolled it out too soon, on someone's orders. Somebody with a favorite team got a real big bug up their— got very annoyed about something, and insisted that this big gun be deployed here and now . . . in a *spatball* tournament?" He shook his head. "I would have waited for the Fantasy Super Bowl. There's real money in that. Spat's barely taken off yet, by comparison." Winters fell silent again.

"But what do we do now?" Catie said. "If we remove the instructions, that's going to be great for South Florida, maybe, but it's a one-time fix. Whoever put the altered instructions there will know we're on to them, and go straight underground. You'll never find out who did it, and they'll just try it again, somewhere else, somewhere that's not as well policed."

"Yes," Winters said, rocking back in his chair. He was silent for a moment, and then finally he said, "Best case would be to let them trigger their 'switch' . . . while we have a tracer routine in place to catch them in the act. If indeed we can install such a thing. If there's time. And assuming it won't somehow invalidate the whole tournament."

Winters sat still, looking into space for a moment. "I think we don't have much choice this time," he said. "We're going to have to call in a big intervention team . . . and Mark as well, I think; his dad won't be wild about it, but even he's going to see the necessity, I would guess. And even with him, and all our best people, this is going to be a mess. A very, very lively day or three."

"Can't you just plug in standard variables to replace the bad ones?" Catie said.

"I wish it were that simple. If there wasn't going to be anyone watching to see whether their carefully installed 'fix' was working properly, I'd say yes. Unfortunately we don't have that option. It's almost certain that they're watching the server closely to see if anyone tampers with it, and it's equally certain that they'll have booby-trapped their own routines to alert them if anyone messes with them. The one good thing is, they'll have been watching our earlier investigation, and will have assumed that we didn't find anything. Correctly." His look was momentarily grim. "It would be nice if that makes them a little careless. But we can't count on that. And meanwhile everything has to seem to be working just as they want it to until the very last minute, until they put their own people in place to throw the switch. . . ."

He fell silent again, musing, for a few moments. Then he looked up at Catie. "On to other things . . . You told me," Winters said, "that your friend's been very cooperative."

"More than that," Catie said. "He knows who I'm working for."

"You didn't tell him—"

"Of course not!" She got control of herself immediately. "But I'm sure he knows, all the same. He's a smart man. And, if the information he's been passing me is any indication, he's absolutely willing to help."

"That's useful," Winters said. "We'll see how useful in a while." He looked up at Catie again. "But the most important thing. He didn't give you any sense that there's anyone on his team who's been involved with this?"

"Not at all."

There was a long silence. "All right," Winters said. "We'll have to take it that way for the moment." He sat back, folding his arms.

"I should say," Catie said, "that I'm sorry."

There was a long silence, one that froze her heart. "Yes," Winters said. "You should."

Catie swallowed.

"A question, though . . . I would have thought," Winters said, "that it was mostly the imagery end of things that you would have been looking at."

"I thought so, too," Catie said. "That's how I started. But it all looked just as it was supposed to. And once I got started, I—"

"Couldn't let it go," Winters said in unison with Catie. She fell silent again.

"Yes," he said. "It's a familiar theme. I have about ten thousand coworkers with the same problem. It has its place. But that urge has to be controlled, that stubbornness, and used wisely, used responsibly." He frowned. "Catie, you overstepped the mark. And more, you may even have manipulated Mark into letting you do it."

"*I* manipulated—?" she started to say, and then stopped herself. *If anyone was doing the manipulating*, she thought, *it was that little Squirt of a Gridley!* But that probably wouldn't have been a tactically advantageous thing to say at this point, even if she could have worked up the nerve.

"Which takes some doing, it has to be admitted," Winters said, in a less annoyed tone of voice. "Mark's precocity tends to blind people to his own weaknesses . . . of which he has a few. But we'll leave that to one side for the moment. The problem right now is to work out what to do with the information you've found. May I use your system to make a couple of calls?"

"Please feel free. Space?"

"Just waiting for you to tell me what to do, boss."

She saw Winters's eyebrows go up. "Please make Mr. Winters a privacy space, and connect to whatever address he asks you for."

"Done."

The air around where Winters was sitting went opaque in the swirling blue pattern that Catie had designed for her mother's "hold" function. For about five minutes she sat there and castigated herself for rampant stupidity, while the blue smoke swirled. Finally it evaporated, and Winters walked out through the blue smokescreen. "Thanks, Catie."

"You can kill that, Space," Catie said.

"Yes, O Mistress of All Reality." The smoke vanished.

Catie scowled, furious. Winters looked startled, and then suddenly started laughing, and didn't stop for some seconds. Catie lost her anger, while at the same time wondering whether she was off the hook.

"This is what you get for letting Mark Gridley near your machinery," James Winters said, when he finally found his breath again. "I wish you luck getting rid of the 'improvements.' "

"I can see where I'm going to need it," Catie said.

Winters looked around him. "You'll forgive me, I hope, if I leave without taking this discussion much further. I have a lot to do. . . . We've got to independently verify what you found in such a way that it can be salvaged as evidence. I may disagree with your methods, but I'm thankful for your findings, you know."

"I understand. I'm sorry I caused you trouble."

"I accept the apology," Winters said. "But, by the way . . . I quote, 'What do we do now?' . . . "

Catie stood silent again, completely nonplussed.

Winters smiled again . . . a small, dry smile that was nonetheless a great relief to Catie. "The attitude," he said, "is possibly an augury of things to come. We'll see how you shape up. Talented image wranglers are valuable, yes. And they're a dime a dozen. But what we can always use are people who're willing to stretch outside their specialty and take a risk because they just can't let the job at hand alone, when they know it has to be done."

Then the smile flashed out fully. "And between you and me," James Winters said, "we can always use people who are followed around by plain dumb luck. There's never enough of that to go around . . . though by itself, it's fairly useless. Even the best bullet needs a gun barrel around it."

Catie nodded.

"Time to get to work," Winters said. "With any kind of luck, someone's knocking on Karen de Beer's door right now, and some of my people are going to be wanting to talk to me shortly."

"Oh, *no* . . . !" Catie said.

"It's all right," Winters said. "She won't be home. What, did you think we were going to sit around and allow her to be intimidated? That the guy shows up is going to be enough for us to act on. George Brickner will certainly testify, later, that he knew about it beforehand. Meanwhile I have other things to do. That server is going to have to be debugged so that the play-offs can go ahead, while still preserving the contaminated version of the code. We've got our work cut out for us, and not a lot of time to get everything done. If in fact it can be done in time at all. Frankly, I have my doubts."

He looked at Catie keenly. "But a question for you before I go. Identify the famous graphic artist responsible for this quote: 'There is hope in honest error . . . none in the icy perfection of the mere stylist.' "

"Uh," Catie said, and then closed her mouth again, becoming suddenly aware that this was not intended merely as a quote.

Winters held up his index finger. "*One* honest error," he said. "All my people know I'll allow them that much. Twice, and you get really yelled at. Make a note."

"Noted," Catie said, in a somewhat strangled voice.

"Thanks, Catie," James Winters said, turned, went hurriedly through the door that opened for him in the middle of the Great Hall, and vanished.

Catie got out of her space, and out of virtuality, and let Hal have the machine without even arguing about it, and went on down to her room and just sat there for a while, with the door shut, feeling terrible. *I can't believe how completely I've screwed everything up!* Yet as a little time passed, and she started to recover from the shock of what had just happened, Catie was forced to admit to herself that the screwup hadn't been total. Winters had actually been slightly pleased with her . . . which, frankly, was a better outcome than she had hoped for. It wasn't that the bouquet he'd handed her hadn't mostly been thorns, but they were ones that she deserved, and the two or three rather shredded blossoms concealed among them were, Catie supposed, worth it in the end.

She came out of hiding after three-quarters of an hour or so, to find her brother still using the Net machine in the family room. Catie knew she was going to have to talk to George Brickner shortly, but she wasn't in any hurry about it. She wanted to make sure her composure was back in place. She rooted around in the fridge briefly, came up with a couple of chicken breasts, and made herself a fast meal that was a favorite of her mother's: the chicken breasts sauteed with butter and a chopped-up onion, and the whole business "deglazed" with balsamic vinegar. In the middle of her cooking, Hal came out of the family room looking slightly glazed himself.

"You seen the news lately?" he said.

Catie shook her head. "I've been busy."

"You'd better go have a look at it."

"Huh? Why?"

"The sports news. Take my word for it."

"What?"

Hal just shook his head. "I'll watch this for you. Go take a look."

She blinked at that, for it was usually hard to stop Hal from giving you a nearly word-by-word narration of what—

ever news he'd heard recently, whether you wanted to hear it or not. Catie handed Hal the spatula with which she had been stirring the sauce around while it boiled down, and went in to sit down in the implant chair again.

Once into the Great Hall, she said, "Space?"

"I told him everything," her workspace manager said. "If you leave now, you may still have time to get out of the country before they seal the borders."

"Thanks loads. CNNSI, please. Sports headlines, rolling. Latest."

A moment later the effusive young guy with the wild hairstyle who was doing afternoon and evening news on CNNSI lately was standing behind a desk in front of Catie. "—In an unusual move apparently made for operational reasons, the International Spatball Federation has changed its scheduling for this year's spatball play-offs." Behind the anchor, the "background" showed an impressive-looking lineup of implant chairs and very high-end Net boxes and terminals. "The management of Manchester United High announced today that software trouble at their newly installed, multimillion-pound Professional Play Center at Anfield has made it impossible for them to meet the originally scheduled play date of this Thursday. Since the ISF was informed within the mandated twelve-hour emergency notification limit, the team will not forfeit its match with the Chicago Fire. That match has been rescheduled to Saturday, and the Saturday match between the South Florida Spat Association and Xamax Zurich has been moved to Thursday evening by agreement with those two teams."

"Oh, *no*," Catie said softly. *They'll never be ready in time.*

Worse. The server will never be debugged in time!

The game is going to have to go ahead . . . and the people who wanted to ruin the Banana Slugs' chances to win are going to do just that—

She came back to herself to hear the sportscaster saying, "—this is the third major software failure in two months to assail the new installation at Anfield, which has been dogged from inception to installation by cost overruns and then by hardware glitches, as well as by problems with the new MaximumVolume software and operating system which was developed for Manchester. The first two failures of the system, late in the 'scheduled' season, caused one forfeit and one loss due to the failure of center forward Alan Bellingham's custom player suite during the third half of United's crucial preplay-off game with Tokyo Juuban and Ottawa. Manchester United shareholders have once again called for an independent inquiry into the team's dealings with sports-simming software giant Camond, the president of the shareholders' association once again asserting that—"

Catie sat there in unbelieving dismay, her dinner forgotten. "Space . . ."

"I was only following orders."

"Yeah, right. Is George Brickner available?"

"Trying his space for you now."

There was a brief pause. "Who's there?"

"It's Catie."

"Oh." Another pause. "Just a minute."

It was more like a couple of minutes. She waited. When he walked into her space, George took one look at the shocked expression on her face, and paused, and then he just nodded. "You heard."

"Yeah."

He sat down in the chair which had been left there for James Winters. She plopped down in the Comfy Chair, but for once it brought her little comfort. "You talked to James Winters. . . ."

"Among various other people," George said, rubbing his face, "yes." He looked very tired.

Catie knew how he felt, all of a sudden. "George, why did you *do* it?"

"Agree to change the schedule, you mean? Because the ISF asked us to. And we didn't have a good reason to say no."

"But you did! If you—"

"Catie," George said, "if we refused to allow the change in schedule—and it was a perfectly reasonable request on the ISF's part—you know what would happen.

People would have started asking questions. Why were we so reluctant? What was going on? And soon enough, someone would have found out. Or else one of the people involved with what was done to the ISF spat-volume server would have started to suspect something . . . and they would all have folded their little operation up and gone into hiding. After all this trouble, nothing would be solved."

It was her own argument, twisted into a horrible shape that she had never imagined, and it stunned Catie into silence. George was quiet for a few moments, too.

"You think I don't know what you're thinking?" George said. "Believe me, I feel the same way. It would have been great to get in there and have a chance at winning this tournament, to do a thing that would make spat-ball history. Even a chance of making it to the semifinals—that would have been something to tell our grandchildren about. But if we don't stop what's happening to spat, stop it right now, there'll be no sport *to* tell our grandchildren about. . . . Not one worth playing, anyway." He swallowed. "Sports is about making sacrifices, sometimes. This is one of those times. The team agrees with me."

"Do they know . . . ?"

He looked at her. "They know enough," George said. "The Net Force people have been in to check their machines. They've been sabotaged, Catie. We can't touch that, either. We can't change *anything*. If we do, the people behind the sabotage will know, and they'll go to ground somewhere. And who knows, maybe we'll win . . . but the sport will lose. And all the people like us who play it for joy, they'll lose, too."

Catie looked at George with an ache in her middle that she couldn't have described in any words. "It's bad enough that you're so good-looking," Catie said after a while, maybe more bitterly than she intended, "but do you have to be a *hero*, too? It's just not fair."

"Things aren't usually," George said. "But there's no harm in trying to make them fair for the next guy along."

Catie could think of no reply to that.

"It's not going to be so bad," George said.

"Yes, it is," said Catie.

George's face twisted into a pained shape Catie didn't particularly like to see on it. "All right," he said, "yes! It *is*! But we can't let that stop us. We're going to give them a fight like they've never seen before. We're going to show the people who put the fix in that the *only* way to stop us is to fix the game in ways that have never been seen before . . . and even if we lose, we're going to play like no one's ever seen a spat team play before. We're going to play so well that everyone who sees the game we're about to lose will shake their heads and wonder what the heck went wrong. Then when they see Chicago play at the weekend, those same people are going to shake their heads and say, 'They should never have made it this far. Someone must have been cheating the system somehow.' And that's the best way for us to respond, the only way that also helps Net Force do what *it* needs to do about this situation. I don't like it much. It's not at all the ending for this season that I dreamed of. The team doesn't like it much, either. It doesn't match *their* dreams. But we're *not* going to go quietly. I promise you that!"

They both sat quiet for a few moments, looking in different directions. Then George looked over at the chessboard. "I see you've got me in a knight fork," he said.

"I've had you there for three moves," Catie said.

"You gonna do anything about it?"

"I've started doing something about it," Catie said. "Your bishop."

"I'm not worried about that," George said, and gave her a superior look. "Not after the way you threw that last knight away. Anyway, I'm going to take your queen in three moves."

"No, you're not," Catie said.

"Yes, I am," George said.

"You can't. There's no way—" Catie got up and stalked over to the chessboard, glad of an excuse not to have to look at George. She was upset; upset at the unfairness of life, which was about to cheat this guy and his friends of a victory that they deserved. And she hated to have people see her when she was upset.

"There," she said, and picked up one of her bishops and moved it. The window hanging in the air with the notation of the game changed itself to reflect the move.

George got up and wandered over to the chessboard, looking over Catie's shoulder at the board's center area. "Getting messy in there," he said.

"Not nearly as messy as some places," Catie said, heartsore. In her mind all she could see was that great piled-up tangle of code in the ISF server, intricate, complex, and rotten at its core.

George was silent for a moment. "Catie," he said. "You did the best you could. It's out of our hands now—your hands and mine. All we can do now is play the game through to the end, and try to do it with some dignity. And in the meantime . . . I appreciate that you were trying to help. I really do."

Catie nodded. "Do you have a move?" she said.

He looked at the board one more time. "Not tonight," he said. "I'll have a couple for you tomorrow, before we go off to practice. And then one more later."

"All right," she said.

George went back to his doorway, went through it, vanished. Catie didn't turn to watch him go, just looked at the bishop she had moved, and found herself suddenly wishing that the game she had so much been looking forward to would never happen at all.

The last contact between them before the game, on Wednesday night, was made over a voice-only line. They would not now speak again until after the game on Thursday.

". . . The neighbors said she left early to pick up her daughter at school," Darjan said, "and she didn't come back. She went off to hide somewhere, apparently. She hasn't come back yet."

"You going to let her get away with that?"

Darjan laughed. "It's not vital. There are four other people being worked on in other cities. We've got other fish to fry, anyway. When they changed the schedule, everybody had to scurry to make sure that the mirror was working right. There'll be some people pleased, anyway. The Slugs'll be out of the running that much faster. How about your end of things? All the South Florida players' servers taken care of?"

"All handled now."

"Fine. Let's go over all the other arrangements one last time."

Heming laughed. "Always the perfectionist, huh, Armin?"

"Always," Darjan said. "Just call me fond of keeping my skin in one piece."

"They don't pay you enough for the amount you worry," Heming said.

"No," said Darjan, "they don't. Let's start at the top. . . ."

8

Despite Catie's preferences, Thursday eventually came. The game was scheduled for nine P.M. Eastern time, and Catie went to her mom and dad to make sure that both the Net machines in the house were going to be available for her and Hal. But her mother and father already knew about the scheduling, and seemed surprised that she was bothering to ask.

"With all the coverage there's been about this in the last couple of days, honey," her mother said, "you know we wouldn't deprive you!" She was unloading another pile of books onto the kitchen table, this batch, from the looks of it, was heavy on the classics again, but mostly sixteenth- and seventeenth-century French literature.

Catie sighed, picking up a copy of *Gargantua and Pantagruel* and paging through it. She hadn't been looking at the spatball coverage. It made her heart ache to think of what was going to happen to South Florida tonight. Mostly she had been catching up on schoolwork and making the occasional chess move to match the two that George had made since she spoke to him last. But those were the only times she'd been online since then.

Her dad wandered through the kitchen then, holding a

package. "Hon, what happened to my knife?"

"Your knife?"

"The one in the studio."

Her mother went over to the dishwasher and pulled out a tired-looking plastic-handled steak knife, and handed it to her father. "I thought I would give it a scrub while its shape could still be made out somewhat under the paint," she said.

"The dishwasher got it this clean?" her dad said, starting to work with the knife on the package he was carrying. "Amazing!"

"No, a hammer and chisel and elbow grease got the first inch of paint off it," her mother said. "Hard work, not a miracle, paid off there. Catie, honey, did I tell you we talked to James Winters again?"

"Again?" Catie put the book down. "What did he want?"

"Just to thank us for letting you help," her father said. "He thinks highly of you."

Catie raised her eyebrows. "It's nice to know," she said.

Her father put the knife down on the table and started peeling open the package. " 'Nice to know'? Have you had a change of career goals all of a sudden?"

"Uh, no . . . I'm just tired." She checked her watch.

"How long is that game, honey?" her mother said.

"About two hours or so, unless they go into overtime."

"All right. As long as I can have one of the machines sometime before bed . . ."

"No problem."

Nine o'clock came soon enough, and Catie took the machine in the family room. Hal took the one down the hall. In the Great Hall she paused to look over the chessboard for any new moves. There were none. "Space . . ."

"You know, you're more beautiful every day."

Catie looked up into the air with a cockeyed expression. "I think I liked it better when you were insulting me."

"You'll probably be sorry you said that in a few years. Was there something you wanted?"

"Friends-and-family space in the ISF spatball volume, please . . ."

A doorway appeared in the middle of the Great Hall. "Any messages waiting?" Catie said before she went through.

"Nothing, boss."

"Okay. Flag me as busy for the next two hours."

She slipped into the microgravity of the friends-and-family space and greeted some of the other team members' relatives whom she knew slightly, then settled down among them. Hal popped in a few minutes later, bubbling over with excitement. "I can't believe it's finally happening," he said. "I can't believe it. . . ."

"I can," Catie said softly.

He turned to look at her. "Cates," he said, "have you and George had a fight or something?"

"It's not me-and-George," Catie said, "and no, we haven't had a fight." *Probably it would be simpler if we had. . . .*

"You sure?"

Catie gave Hal a don't-push-your-luck look . . . then felt guilty and softened her expression. "Yeah, I'm sure. Why?"

"It's just that if he said something that bothered you," Hal said, "I was going to adjust his attitude."

Catie had to laugh at that. "It's nothing like that," she said. "But look . . . thanks anyway."

"Uh-oh," Hal said. "Here we go . . . !"

The cheering was beginning as the players from both sides, Xamax in their green and white, South Florida in their yellow and black, were floating into the volume now, taking positions around the walls as the environment announcer read out their names and numbers to the usual wild cheers. The captains came last, as always. When George's name was announced, the usual cry of "Par*rot*! Par*rot*!" went up from the South Florida fans all around. George looked over toward the F&F space and lifted a hand to wave. Every relative and friend in the place cheered and waved back, Catie included, but Catie knew whom he had been looking at, with a slighly somber gaze, and knew what the message was. *We will* not *go quietly, I promise you!*

After the national anthems Catie sat through the first
and second halves with little enthusiasm . . . or tried to.
Around the middle of the second half, she found that the
sheer élan with which South Florida was playing started
to break her mood, which even the screaming and holler-
ing of the fans gathered around the Slugs' friends-and-
family area hadn't been able to do. Xamax was a good
team, very good indeed. Over time they had carefully se-
lected and recruited some of the best players in Europe.
Then (for reasons Catie didn't understand in the slightest)
they had sent out for a famous English spatball coach who
had been with Man United for a while, and who now
shouted at his players from the outer shell in either a hilarious Midlands-accented form of Swiss German that
made him sound like he had a throat disease, or a really
barbarous French that sounded like someone gargling with
Channel water. Whatever they thought of his accents, his
players loved the man and played their hearts out for him.

But they didn't play like the Slugs. *Will it make a difference at this level?* Catie had asked, and now she realized how dumb the question had been. The team's
friendship, their relationship, turned them into the closest
thing to a bunch of spatball-playing telepaths that Catie
had ever seen. They all seemed to know where they all
were almost without looking. They passed and played, not
like separate people, but like parts of the same organism.
And they were not playing for a coach, however beloved,
but for each other. It made a difference, all right.

The trouble was that, at the end of the third half, it still
wasn't going to matter. At the end of the second half the
score was already 3–2–0, and Catie knew that this was
just an early indicator of the way the game would end.
Already she had seen two goals which seemed to happen
faster than any she had ever seen, situations where the
balls had seemed almost to swerve on their way through
the volume, as if the law of gravity had suddenly shifted
in the spatball's neighborhood, and the Slugs, even playing at their best as they plainly were, couldn't cope. It
was a lost cause, made more poignant because they just
would not give up, would not play as if it was anything

but a championship game. George had been right. They were playing out of their skins, out of their hearts, going for broke.

He's not the only hero out there, Catie thought as the horn went for the end of the second half.

"It's not over yet," Hal was saying as the teams went out of the volume for their final break. "Only one more goal to draw—"

Catie shook her head. "I know," she said. She also knew that it wasn't going to happen. But her mood was changing. Heroism was worth honoring, even if there wasn't a win in prospect. Playing the game as if it mattered . . . that in itself, in a situation like this, was a win of sorts, though maybe not the kind that the world would recognize. Catie knew. George knew, too, and his team knew—

Where the next twenty minutes went, Catie had no idea. The teams came back into the spat volume at the end of break, the referee and the invigilator gave one another the thumbs-up, and the third half began. And if she thought she had seen committed, ferocious play before, Catie realized that she hadn't seen any such thing. War broke out in the spat volume: a graceful, low-gravity war, in which there seemed to be an agreement not to kill or seriously injure anyone—but war nonetheless.

"Injuries" began to pile up. South Florida lost two players to injury-level wall impacts almost within the first ten minutes, and Xamax lost three, so that they had to send in a replacement forward, one of only two they had left. The play got a little more cautious after that, as Xamax had no desire whatsoever to fall below minimum number and reduce its lead to a draw—there was no forfeiting for below-minimum situations when only two teams were playing. But George continued to play his team as if there was a war on, and Catie knew why, if no one else in the "arena" did—South Florida had nothing to lose. The crowd was beginning to react to the sense of urgency that was radiating from the spat volume. From all around her, from fans of both stripes, the screaming never stopped. If Catie thought she had heard it get loud at a spatball game before, now she realized that she hadn't heard anything—and indeed, if this hadn't been a virtual experience, when she got out of it she *wouldn't* have heard anything. Her ears would have been ringing for a good while.

Thirty minutes of play reduced themselves to twenty, and twenty to ten, and ten to five, and the two teams were still hammering at each other as if the fate of civilizations rested on who won this game. Once South Florida almost scored, but somehow a Xamax player rocketed into the ball's path from what seemed an impossible distance, blocking the ball away from a goal where the goalie was briefly absent; and at the same time, the goal precessed (it seemed to Catie) a lot sooner than it should have. The South Florida fans roared disappointment. That was the only time when the tears actually sprang to Catie's eyes at the unfairness of it all—that people should play like this against malign and invisible forces, and have no real win to show at the end of it, nothing concrete to match the unquestionable moral victory. *The moral victory's going to have to do. But all the same, it's just a shame—*

Next to her, Hal was shaking with excitement. Catie glanced at the clock. Four minutes left. It was too much to hope for a miracle at this point, and anyway, there were forces operating behind the scenes to prevent any miracle from taking place. At three and a half minutes South Florida began lining up another play on the present Xamax goal, a long pass around the perimeter. Catie shook her head. She had seen too many of these fail in the last two halves, as goals seemed to precess out of sequence, the ball refused to go where it was supposed to—

"Catie!"

Not Hal . . . somebody on her right. Catie turned and saw that Mark Gridley was suddenly there. "Huh?" she said. "Where'd *you* come from?"

"Where you think."

"I couldn't stop him, boss," her workspace manager whispered in her ear. "He overrode me to get your coordinates, the brute."

Catie sighed and shook her head again. "How's it going?"

"It's not 'going.' It *went*."

"You get cryptic at the most inconvenient times," Catie said, turning her attention back to the spat volume. "Save it for later, Squirt. We're at the end of a game here, they're losing and you know why. Can't you—"

"No, they're not."

She looked at him, confused. "But, the—Mark, the code—it's, you know—"

"No, it's not. It's clean."

And he started to laugh. "It's *clean*, Catie! This is for real!"

"It's—you mean they're *not*—"

"It's been clean since the start of the game. I was held up, we had to—"

"You mean they can—*OH MY GOSH*" They can actually win, *oh, no, oh, my*—

"*Go, SLUGS!*" Catie yelled at the top of her voice, the sheer volume of it nonetheless becoming almost lost in the sea of sound all around her. *They have a chance to win. They actually have a chance!*

And now it was as if the whole game had been different from the beginning . . . and now the ending mattered more than ever. The whole arena had become a generator of a single nonstop cheer which was now indistinguishable from white noise, a noise that was "white" the way the sun is white. Catie was as much part of it now as anyone else was. *I'll be hoarse tomorrow,* she thought, and didn't care in the slightest. That long pass that South Florida was setting up came apart as Villeneuve from Xamax snagged it behind a knee, between Daystrom and Marcus, and made off with it. In possession now, Xamax made it plain that they intended to stay that way until time ran out. But the Slugs had other plans. They bounced off the walls and off each other and off the Xamax players in ways that even George and Gracie's kids had never thought of, and in the middle of them, receiving and passing, and receiving and passing again, there was Brickner, unstoppable, until the Xamax players tried informally to scrum him just to keep him out of the way.

Two minutes. There was no way it could continue at

this level, but it continued. Somehow George was no longer at the center of that scrum. He found daylight, emerged into it with the ball in the crook of one elbow, flung the ball to his cocaptain. Mike caught it in a knee-bend, rolled like lightning in yaw axis, flung it away to Daystrom. She caught it elbow-wise, passed it, had it passed back to her. Lined up on the goal—

The goal precessed. The roar, impossibly, got louder. One minute. Daystrom pushed herself off an unfortunate Xamax blocker, spun in pitch axis, fired the ball away again. Someone else from Xamax snagged it, began again the game of keep-away, the only goal to keep South Florida from scoring. Pass, pass, pass, into a self-inflicted scrum and (theoretically) out the other side—except that somehow a South Florida team member, one of the flankers, Monahan, managed to work one arm into that scrum and somehow come out with the ball. The crowd's noise got impossibly louder. Now the passing game started again, and the Xamax players got busy covering the goals. Thirty seconds. A few of them made attempts to get the ball away from the Slugs again, but their captain shouted them back to the goals again. If they were properly covered there was no danger, nothing to do but wait for time to run out. Twenty seconds.

The goals precessed another hex along. The pass came to Daystrom. She fired it like a bullet at George Brickner. George snagged it, spun, and if it came to him like a bullet, it left him like a laser beam, straight and almost impossible to see, fired right at one of the goals, at a patch of daylight between two of the Xamax guards.

One of them moved just enough to block it. It bounced into the center of the volume again, and George snagged it one more time, pushed off the nearby Daystrom, spun for impetus, and fired it back the way it had come.

The Xamax guard blocked it again. It bounced right back at George. He passed to Daystrom, pushing off her as he did so. She tumbled, came around, fired the ball at him one last time. He caught it, spinning, feinted at the Xamax blocker, threatening a third attempt—spun again, feinted as if to pass, spun—

The ball left him one last time, straight for the goal. The Xamax blocker had drifted just a little to one side. . . .

The horn went.

The spatball impacted squarely in the center of the goal hex.

Amid the impossible roaring, Catie gasped for breath, and wondered when she had last had one.

The occupants of both F&F spaces were emptying into the spat volume now. Hal plunged past her, and Catie, wrung out, astonished, saddened but somehow still delighted, went after him. All the players were being mobbed, jerseys were being torn off and flung around, and the final result was flashing in the scoring hexes now: 3–2–0, Xamax.

Catie was out of practice in microgravity, but all the same she found a patch of daylight in one particular mob, and worked her way through it. There was George, still in possession of his jersey.

Catie threw her arms around him and hugged him hard.

He held her away, and grinned at her. It was not an expression of perfect joy by any means. There was pain there. But there was also profound satisfaction . . . and a touch of mischief.

"You knew," she said. "You *knew!*"

"Gotcha," said George.

Catie began to pummel him as unmercifully as if he'd been her brother. But it didn't last. His teammates and their families and other hangers-on seized George and propelled him toward the suddenly open side of the spat volume, chanting "Par*rot!* Par*rot!* Par*rot!*"—making for the locker room in triumph, as if South Florida had won.

But then, Catie thought, as she went along with them, *in every way that counts most it has* . . .

Much later, in the locker room, when all possible interviews had been given, and everybody from the media had been evicted, well soaked with virtual champagne, and when the space had been sealed and the outer shell of the virtual environment encrypted, they came face-to-face again.

"You knew," Catie said again.

"Of course I knew," George said. "But I couldn't tell you."

"There wasn't time," Mark Gridley said, appearing from one side, "and my dad made him agree not to tell. *I* wanted to tell you, but my dad—"

"Threatened his life," said a voice that Catie didn't recognize. "Occasionally it has an effect."

Catie turned around and saw a handsome man of Thai ancestry, in casual clothes: a man with an unsurprising resemblance to Mark. Jay Gridley, the director of Net Force, came over to George Brickner and stuck his hand out. "That was one hell of a game," he said.

"Thanks," George said, and shook Gridley's hand. "Champagne?"

"Inside, not outside, please. Not that it takes more than an eyeblink's time to change clothes on the virtual side of things, but I have a lot of work left to do tonight, and once I've been drenched in any kind of champagne, real or unreal, it seems to remove my administrative edge."

Someone found Jay a glass. He lifted it in an informal toast to George and his team, and drank.

Catie, meanwhile, had turned to Mark. "If you don't tell me what you guys did," Catie said, "I'm going to do a lot more more than threaten your life."

"The players' own machines were the easy part," Mark said. "Net Force teams got at them all quietly over the past few days and put in 'transparent' routers to other Net boxes, circumventing the local sabotage. But there was still the ISF server to deal with. Since time was so limited, the best course of action seemed to be to set up another spat server, a substitute, using the ISF's own licensed software. Then we completely duplicated the tampered ISF server to it. After that, we debugged the code in the original server. We were up all night." Not that there was any way to tell this by looking at Mark. He was flushed with triumph, a triumph that had a wicked edge to it. "We finished about two and a half hours ago. But there was still more to do, then. The ISF had convened its server certification people in secret. They came in and checked the duplicate server over, and certified it. Finished up twenty minutes before the game, while the pregame show was still running."

"Geez," Catie said. "But how did they—? The certification procedures—I thought you had to—"

"Check every line of code by human oversight? No machines? Yeah. It was close. There was not a single Net Force geek who slept last night, anywhere on the planet." Mark grinned. "There are a lot of spatball fans on the Force. . . ."

Catie considered all this. "So the bad guys, the people who had installed the false variables in the usual server . . ."

". . . Thought they were operating on the usual server, where gameplay was taking place," Jay Gridley said. "But they were actually operating on the dupe . . . into which we simply mirrored the genuine gameplay. By the time they realized their mistake, it was too late for them. We had a complete set of tracer routines installed in the mirror. There were three different people handling the switching variables, one in Portland, one in Beijing, and one in Auckland. All representatives of the major illegal betting syndicates . . . all of them now helping us with our inquiries."

"It was a variation of their own trick," Catie said softly. "You just turned it around and used it against them!"

" 'Own goal,' " Mark said. "They did it to themselves . . . with a vengeance." He grinned.

"Ah, the conquering heroes," said another voice. James Winters had slipped in and found himself a glass of the virtual champagne. Now he strolled over to them.

"Heroes, yes," George said, looking around at his teammates. "Conquering?"

"Eveything's relative," Winters said. "I think the epithet fits today. Meanwhile," he said to Jay Gridley, "everything at the software and hardware end is handled; the original server, the contaminated routines, and the duplicates are all locked down. We can start getting the prosecuting team pulled together tomorrow. How about the other operation?"

"Handled," Jay said, and looked over at George. "This is the other piece of news you need to hear. A gentleman named Darjan, Armin Darjan, got himself a flat tire in the middle of I-95 just outside Miami Tuesday afternoon. Seems he'd just been to see one of the South Florida team members, but he didn't find her at home. The Miami police helped him get over to the hard shoulder, but while they were taking his particulars and helping him call a tow truck, one of them noticed something in his rental car that shouldn't have been there. They brought him into the local police station to talk to him about it, and when he realized what the penalty is in Florida for carrying that particular weapon, especially without a concealed-carry permit, he became fairly talkative."

George smiled slightly. "He seems to have a lot of friends in the computer-service business," Gridley said. "Not to mention a lot of friends in financial circles, here and overseas. He talked to the police about all kinds of things, and when they got the gist of what was going on, they called us. We had a long talk with him, too, and took his prints and his passport from him, and called him a lawyer . . . and then we told him what he had to do over the next couple of days to make sure that the plea the lawyer was going to cut for him would stay in the same shape after this game as before. He was *most* cooperative."

"Lucky he had that flat tire right then," Catie said, feeling fairly daring to just come out and say what she was thinking to the head of Net Force.

"Heaven forbid I should complain," Gridley said, his face perfectly straight. "It might make someone in local law enforcement think we were ungrateful."

There were smiles all around at that. "So, ladies and gentlemen," Gridley said to the South Florida team members gathered around, "thank you for your help. Some of you will be hearing from us in the very near future as we pursue this matter. Meanwhile, I'm sorry you didn't win."

"We're not," somebody said, and popped another bottle

of champagne. "It means we can party *now*!"

This sentiment was met with much cheering. "Meanwhile," Jay Gridley said, turning to Catie, and grabbing his son in a friendly way behind the neck as he did so, "please tell me if there's anything you feel you need removed from your workspace manager."

"Uh, I'll think about it and let you know," Catie said. "The present configuration has a sort of strange amusement value."

"*Strange* would be the word," Gridley said. "Come on, Mark. Good night, Catie, and thanks again."

The Gridleys vanished.

A little later Catie found her way back to George again. "One thing," she said, "before I turn in. You knew that I was helping Net Force from the very start, didn't you."

"I suspected," George said. "Very strongly. I mean, you practically had it painted on your forehead."

Catie blushed. She thought she had been fairly circumspect.

"But I wasn't going to say anything out loud," George said. "I wasn't sure how carefully the 'eavesdroppers' might have been listening to me . . . and I didn't want to get anyone else in trouble."

Catie nodded. "There's just one more thing," she said. "Yes?"

"Even though the server was clean . . . you lost."

George nodded, looking completely unconcerned. "They're a good team," he said. "They deserved to win. Anybody who could play us the way we were playing today, and win, is unquestionably championship material." He smiled, a rather more reflective look. "And South Florida's made a little history today. We've never gotten this far before. So, next year . . ."

"Next year," Catie said. "By then you'll be a professional. My prediction."

"Interesting," George said. "We'll see."

"And famous."

"I'm famous now," George said mildly. "For whatever that's worth." He looked around him. "But with people like this around me, to be famous *with*, it might be worth something. We'll see."

"All right. But about that chess game—"

"Give me a night off," George said. "If only to recover. Not to mention to consider my next move."

"Okay," Catie said. She glanced over at Hal and made a let's-go-home gesture. He nodded.

"Congratulations," Catie said softly.

George nodded, somber. "Thanks."

And Catie gathered up Hal and left.

The next morning, very early, Catie slipped into her version of the Great Hall of the Library of Congress, with the pink of dawn just coming in through the high windows at the top of the dome, and looked around at the canvases and paperwork lying around the Comfy Chair, still badly in need of sorting. She looked particularly at the e-mails, but there were no new ones.

So now that he's famous, she thought, *is he still talking to me . . . ?*

She turned around and looked at the chessboard, then glanced up at the text window above it, where a line of text was flashing. It read:

    18   PxQ   ch –

And then, out of the air, a voice said: "Gotcha."

Very slowly, Catie smiled.

VIRTUAL CRIME. REAL PUNISHMENT.

TOM CLANCY'S NET FORCE®

Created by Tom Clancy and Steve Pieczenik
written by Bill McCay

*The Net Force fights all criminal activity online. But a group of teen experts
knows just as much about computers as their adult superiors.
They are the Net Force Explorers...*

**Available wherever books are sold or to order call
1-800-788-6262**

B613

From the #1 *New York Times*
Bestselling Phenomenon

Tom Clancy's
NET FORCE

Created by Tom Clancy and Steve Pieczenik
written by Steve Perry

**Virtual crime.
Real punishment.**

Tom Clancy's Power Plays

Created by Tom Clancy and Martin Greenberg
written by Jerome Preisler

TOM CLANCY'S POWER PLAYS: Politika

0-425-16278-8

TOM CLANCY'S POWER PLAYS: ruthless.com

0-425-16570-1

TOM CLANCY'S POWER PLAYS: Shadow Watch

0-425-17188-4

TOM CLANCY'S POWER PLAYS: Bio-Strike

0-425-17735-1

TOM CLANCY'S POWER PLAYS: Cold War

0-425-18214-2

TOM CLANCY'S POWER PLAYS: Cutting Edge

0-425-18705-5

AVAILABLE WHEREVER BOOKS ARE SOLD
OR TO ORDER CALL:
1-800-788-6262

B677